THE SOONER SPY

THE
SOONER
SPY

JIM
LEHRER

Council Oak Books
Tulsa

Council Oak Books
Tulsa, Oklahoma 74120

Originally published by G.P. Putnam's Sons
©1990 by Jim Lehrer. All rights reserved
Council Oak paperback edition published in 1997
01 00 99 98 97   5 4 3 2 1

Library of Congress Cataloging-in-Publication Data

Lehrer, James.
The sooner spy/ Jim Lehrer.
p.   cm.
I. Title.
PS3562.E4419S66   1989   89-38737 CIP
813'.54—dc 20

ISBN 1-57178-041-6

Printed in the United States of America

Cover Design by Scott Warren

To John, Kate and Luke

• • •

·1·

The Hugotown Hug

OBI DIRECTOR C. Harry Hayes was clearly angry with me, his best friend in the government of Oklahoma. He took me right into the Electronic Surveillance Control and Service Room, which stood behind a locked, unmarked and mostly unknown gray door in the rear of his headquarters on 36th Street. We took seats in the back behind a console of tape machines and telephones and lights and buttons. OBI special agent Wilson (Smitty) Smith was seated in front of it.

"You really ought to quit taping everything you do," I said to C. as we sat down, trying to be friendly. "Look what taping did to Nixon."

"I'm not taping conversations about hush money and women's parts in wringers," he said. Matter-of-factly. Not very friendly. "It's like dialing nine-one-one for a fire truck. Everybody who calls here gets recorded."

He nodded to Smitty. In stereo came the recorded voices of C. and another man I did not recognize. They were talking on the telephone.

"This is your friendly spook," said the other man. "How's law enforcement's famous one-eared man?" There was a twang there. Arkansas, I figured. Maybe Louisiana. There was also age and smarts that he must have picked up somewhere else. Plus some mischief.

C. said: "What's up, Colley?"

"What's up is your last good ear, I'm afraid," said the other man.

"Mmmm?"

" 'Mmmm' is right. You remember our lost friend down in the lower east quadrant of your beloved Sooner State?"

"Mmmm uh."

" 'Mmmm uh.' Well, I just hung up from talking to him. He was concerned, C. Seems as though an unusual man was down there watching things yesterday. He was afraid this unusual man might know more than he should know and that if he knew more, then maybe some of his own old, *old* friends might also know more than they should know. I asked him to describe the car and the man. He's an old pro, as you know, C. He had a name for the man, and for cross-checking he had the license number, the make and model of the car. The ID was especially easy because the unusual man was one-eyed. The name he gave me was of a somewhat prominent one-eyed man who is a state officeholder in your state who is also the husband of a prominent businesswoman who franchises drive-thru grocery stores. I also remembered that this somewhat prominent one-eyed man is a close buddy of law enforcement's somewhat famous one-eared man, C.

Harry Hayes. And then, lo and behold, the license check came back with the same name."

"Mmmmm."

"Yeah, 'Mmmmm.' One more lo and behold. My friend said that same unusual somewhat prominent one-eyed man showed up at his Rotary Club but ran like a goosed virgin when he saw him."

"Mmmmmm."

"What's going on, C.?"

"Nothing to worry about, I'm sure. Probably has to do with the wife's business connection . . ."

" 'Nothing to worry about, I'm sure.' Well, fine. But just the same, I'm catching a five-fifteen Braniff from Love Field. Arrives Oke City at six-oh-five. Flight two twenty-three. I'd appreciate your meeting me. We'll have a good dinner. You might want to invite your somewhat prominent friend."

"Sure thing."

" 'Sure thing.' Speaking of sure things, C. If you have blown this little deal, do you know what I am going to do to you?"

There was a pause for an answer that did not come.

The other man continued: "Well. My grandmother on my father's side in Camden, Arkansas, had a most exciting way to kill chickens for dinner. She grabbed them by the head and twirled them around and around in the air until the head was separated from the rest of the chicken. The bottom part of the chicken ran around in circles in the backyard before finally quieting down and dying. It was an awful thing to watch."

"My mother on my side in Durant, Oklahoma, still does it that way."

"Good. You know all about it, then. Good. Because if you and your somewhat prominent one-eyed friend have fouled up our supersensitive situation I may find it necessary to grab you by that one remaining good ear of yours and twirl you around and around in the air until it comes off in my hand."

"I'll see you at the airport at six-oh-five," C. said. "I'll be the naked man carrying a copy of *The Daily Oklahoman* under my left arm. Ask the directions to the National Motorcoach Hall of Fame. I will give the password 'Psycho.' You countersign with 'Spook.' "

"Mmmmm," said the other man.

Special Agent Smith switched off the tape. And left the room.

I, the somewhat prominent one-eyed state officeholder, asked C., law enforcement's somewhat famous one-eared man, to tell me exactly who this man Colley was.

"He's exactly CIA, Mack," C. replied. "He works out of an office across from the post office in Dallas."

"Mmmmm," I replied.

"Why did you go to Utoka, Mack?"

"Relax, C.," I replied. "I just wanted to see for myself what a real Russian spy looked like."

I ended up seeing for myself a lot more than just a Russian spy.

It began two weeks earlier, with my commencement address at Oklahoma Southeastern State College in Hugotown. Buffalo Joe Hayman, our governor, had originally been scheduled to make the speech but he faked the flu so he could send me in his place. The reason was Miss Country

Music of America and the Free World, Nita Pickens of Perkins Corner, Oklahoma. She was a graduate of OSSC, and Buffalo Joe discovered she was going to be honored as the Distinguished Alumnus of the Year at the commencement ceremonies. Unfortunately, Nita Pickens had come back to Oklahoma from Nashville and New York or wherever the year before to support Buffalo Joe's opponent in the Democratic primary. The opponent, a long-hair in his twenties, was her brother-in-law, and he got less than twenty percent of the vote. But that didn't matter to Joe. He was a man of postelection principles and he was a man who repeated himself for emphasis. He said to me: "A politician who lets bygones be bygones ends up being gone himself, Mack. Gone himself. A politician who holds no grudges ends up holding no office. No office at all. A politician who doesn't remember his enemies ends up with nothing much else to remember. Do you understand, Mack?" Joe was famous for his sayings.

The commencement was outside, in the center of the football field where the Oklahoma Southeastern Bobcats played their games. There was a stage for us dignitaries and a thousand or so folding chairs for the 182 graduates and their families and friends. It was a glorious Oklahoma May day, the kind Nita Pickens once described in a song as having the sun as bright as a new Pontiac, the air as sweet as Hilton Hotel soap.

Nita was first. She was bright and sweet, as well as short, red-headed, jumpy nervous and about twenty-seven years old. The president of OSSC and the chairman of the alumni association bestowed upon her the Distinguished Alumnus Award, which was a wooden plaque in the shape of a bobcat head with an engraved piece of gold tacked in the middle. They said she was the youngest person ever to receive the award.

"Thank you, friends and fellow Bobcats," Nita Pickens of Perkins Corner said into the microphone. I heard the sound of a chord being struck on a piano. I saw her begin to snap her fingers and move her butt from side to side. And then came that renowned and admired country voice of hers singing "Hugotown Hug," the song that had catapulted her and her college town to the top of the C&W charts and to fame and stardom.

> *"I'm a lonesome honey from Hugotown*
> *Who wants her Hugotown Hug tonight.*
> *The Hugotown Hug, oh, the Hugotown Hug,*
> *No hug hurts like the Hugotown Hug.*
>
> *"I'm a crying baby from Hugotown*
> *Who needs a Hugotown Hug tonight.*
> *The Hugotown Hug, oh, the Hugotown Hug,*
> *No hug squeezes like the Hugotown Hug."*

The tune was a cross between the fifties favorite "Lovesick Blues" and "Jesus Loves Me." And we all knew it by heart. The president of Oklahoma Southeastern and I and everyone else on that field jumped to their feet and clapped and sang along. The *Hugotown News-Herald* later called it a historic occasion.

And I had to follow this historic occasion with my speech. I was introduced as an inspiration to all young people. Someone who had stood with Governor Hayman and the Oklahoma legislature in keeping OSSC fully funded and accredited. Someone who loved Oklahoma as much as a native in spite of having been born in Kansas. Someone who recognized and loved a Bobcat when he saw one. Someone who had overcome physical harm and maiming to rise to the top of our Sooner government, to a position that was literally a heartbeat away from the *very* top. Someone who was known for his provocative and entertaining speeches a la Will Rogers.

I stood up to a small round of applause. Being the lieutenant governor of Oklahoma meant tremendous rewards and awards. But being recognized and known by the ordinary Sooner citizen was not one of them. When the CIA man on that tape called me somewhat prominent he was giving me all the breaks. I was not à la Will Rogers or à la anything like that. Lieutenant governors are seldom seen, heard or recognized. That is not a complaint. I was honored to be what Joe Hayman called the Second Man of Oklahoma. My story was a true up-from-nowhere story. I had wandered from Kansas to Adabel, Oklahoma, as a young man and through several strokes of luck got elected county commissioner. I came to the attention of some people in the high reaches of the state Democratic Party who chose me for the ticket. I was chosen on an emergency basis after two earlier selectees had to step aside for personal reasons. One had not filed income tax returns for several years; the other had impregnated a constituent other than his wife. I loved being lieutenant governor. But it meant, as now, gazing out on a crowd of people with confused looks of disappointment on their faces. Who is this guy? The lieutenant governor of what? Where's the governor? Wasn't he supposed to be here? Who is this guy? What's he got to say? Who is this guy? Where's the governor?

I really was a pretty fair public speaker. Not because of anything other than having inherited a deep-well voice from my dad and thinking long and hard about what I was going to say before I said it. Commencement addresses were the hardest. People don't come to a kid's graduation—their kid's or somebody else's—to hear the speaker. Nobody cares what is said no matter who says it. With a gun to my head I could not have told anybody what my high school and junior college commencement speakers even looked like, much less what they said.

I talked about the need not to consider yourself well educated. Ever. To always keep reading and listening and have your mind open to new ideas. I said it was important not to get so wrapped up in making a living and going to the bank that you miss the sunsets and the roses, the smell of alfalfa and the laughter of babies, the grins of strangers and the cries of friends, the delight of a cheeseburger all the way and the crack of a bat against a well-thrown baseball.

I wrapped it up with these memorable words:

"As you search for your place in life I hereby advise you to take risks. Be willing to put your mind and your spirit, your time and your energy, your stomach and your emotions on the line.

"To search for a safe place is to search for an end to a rainbow that you will hate once you find it.

"Take charge of your own life. Create your own risks by setting your own standards, satisfying your own standards. Take charge.

"Congratulations to you all. It is unlikely that any of you

will have occasion to remember either me or my commencement address. I don't blame you. But if by chance
something does linger, I hope it's just that there was a one-
eyed guy up here who kept saying, 'Risk. Risk. The way to
happiness is to risk it.'

"Risk it."

I got a good minute and a half of solid applause. Nita
Pickens of Perkins Corner stood up and shook my right
hand as I returned to my seat. "Nobody's ever said it better,
Mr. Lieutenant Governor," she said. "I'm going to dedicate
my next song to you. I'll call it, 'Risk It, O Baby of Mine.' "

The 182 graduates then came one by one in alphabetical
order in their dark purple robes and caps to receive a diploma
and a handshake from the president of OSSC. A Church of
the Holy Road preacher from Davis gave the benediction,
and the ceremonies were over.

We went from the stage in procession to the gym to return
our own dark purple robes. Then we went back out into
the sunshine for a reception.

"Your speech was Boomer Sooner," said the president as
we moved to form a receiving line with Nita Pickens of
Perkins Corner and a few others. "I have never heard a
commencement speech so fine, so memorable, so important,
so innovative, so special, so wrestling." Wrestling? You
mean like two guys in tights on a mat? He was a sandy-
haired man of fifty who wore glasses with tinted lenses and
silver rims. Like he was a crop-duster pilot. Or insurance
adjuster.

I know it is not fair to make general statements about
kinds of people but I must say I had never met a college
president who was completely normal. I don't know if they

go into the job that way or the job itself turns them. Buffalo Joe also had some very funny, mostly obscene things to say about college presidents, particularly around budget submission time. I will not repeat them here.

The next fifty minutes were glorious. I smiled modestly and shook hands with graduates and their families and friends as they, each in their own glorious way, told me how wonderful my speech had been. Show me somebody who says he can't stand compliments for fifty minutes and I'll show you somebody who has never been paid compliments for fifty minutes. Or, in the words of Buffalo Joe: "There's no such thing as modesty, Mack. It's like a haircut. It doesn't exist. It does not exist."

The last person to go through the receiving line was a well-dressed young man who grabbed my right hand and looked right into my one good eye. He was dark-skinned and black-haired. Indian. Probably Choctaw. A third of the graduating class and the student body were Indians.

"That was a brilliant speech, Mr. Lieutenant Governor," he said. His English was perfect. I didn't remember him specifically from the line of graduates, but people look different in dark robes and graduate hats with tassels.

"Thank you," I said modestly.

"But it does not work," he said deadly seriously. Deadly seriously. "I have already tried your Risk It approach and it does not work."

The president, Nita Pickens of Perkins Corner and the others in the receiving line began to drift away. I wanted to drift away as well. I had a two-hour drive back to Oklahoma City. My son, Tommy Walt, said he had something of crucial private importance to discuss with me. I also wanted some of the fruit punch and cookies before I hit the road.

"I'm sorry to hear that," I said to the young Choctaw. "Very sorry."

"I want to put my mind and spirit, my time and energy, my stomach and emotions on the line. But they will not let me."

"Who won't let you?"

"The Central Intelligence Agency."

"Excuse me?"

"The Central Intelligence Agency. I have trained myself to be a spy, an intelligence agent. I want to risk my life and my future for my country. I want to do what you said. But they won't let me."

"Well, I am sorry to hear that," I said, as if we were talking about the possibility of thundershowers in the five-day forecast. I was thinking, Why is there one of these guys in every crowd and why didn't I leave fifteen minutes earlier, but what I said was, "Come by my office if you're ever in Oklahoma City. I'll show you the capitol." It was one of my standard lieutenant governor's lines, and to my relief, it seemed to satisfy him.

"Thank you, sir," he said, and turned away.

I headed for the fruit punch and cookies.

And for very big trouble.

I do not believe in telepathy. I do not believe in any of those crazy things by which people talk to other people, dead or alive, without really talking to them. But I do know that Tommy Walt had not been in one of those folding chairs listening to my Risk It commencement address and that I had never, ever talked to him about what I was going to say or what I even thought about taking risks.

I also know that the first important thing he said to me that evening was:

"I want to go out on my own, Dad. I'm getting too comfortable with Mom at JackieMart. I'm old enough, and if I don't do it now I'm afraid I never will."

We were in his yellow Pontiac Trans Am sports car on the way to Chiquita & Ralph's, the finest Tex-Mex place in Oklahoma City. He was driving. I was in the front passenger seat.

" 'Own'?" was the only reaction that came out of my mouth.

"Own business. I want to start and own my own business."

"You don't like the drive-thru grocery business?"

"I love it. But it's Mom's. It's her creation. I want my own creation."

Tommy Walt. Oh, my dear Tommy Walt. He tried to be a baseball player because I wanted him to, but his body and his fingers were too small and he couldn't hit a curve. He spent several months checking bags at the Union Bus Station in Oklahoma City because I wanted him to have a career in the bus industry. He quit that to join Jackie at JackieMarts Inc. There were only four JackieMarts when he came on board as manager of JackieMart–South Broadway. Now there were fourteen and there was talk of even more. There was always talk of even more with Jackie and her JackieMarts, the first drive-thru grocery stores in America. They were based on her simple idea that people don't like to get out of their cars just to buy a loaf of bread, a carton of milk and other simple basics of life.

"You have become a real linchpin in her operation," I said. "She tells me all the time how your taking charge of franchise relations has meant everything."

"I appreciate that. But I want to work for myself."

"Have you got something in mind?"

"Yes, sir. A restaurant grease collection business."

I looked around at him. For a smile. For some sign he was joking. There was no smile. He was not joking.

"Did you say 'restaurant grease collection'?" I said.

"Yes, sir."

"Why in the world would restaurants give up their grease, and why in the world would anybody else want it if they did, and why in the world would you wish to collect it if they did?"

"The restaurants are through with it. They used to just throw it away but now it's collected and sold to rendering plants. They use it for making soap and things. It's a form of recycling. A great form. I can make good money being the one who collects it and delivers it."

Chiquita and Ralph of Chiquita & Ralph's were Chiquita and Ralph Snider. She was in charge of the food and he was the out-front host and greeter. They had met and married in Harlingen, Texas, where he was a U.S. Air Force hydraulic pump mechanic and she was in high school. They had come to Oklahoma City in 1964 and started their restaurant. Ralph was from Kingfisher, a little place northwest of the city, so it was a natural move. When they started, it was just a six-stool, five-booth hole-in-the-wall a block west from the bus depot. But it flowered and grew and now was Oklahoma City's best, biggest and busiest Tex-Mex restaurant. Those who seemed to know said that was mainly because Ralph and Chiquita were both always there. They trusted nobody but Chiquita and Ralph to run a restaurant called Chiquita & Ralph's.

Ralph always wore a dark blue suit and red tie; his dark gray-brown hair was slicked back and his hands were out shaking others and pounding backs and moving tables and chairs around and passing out menus. And he always made a to-do over us, the somewhat prominent lieutenant governor of Oklahoma and his son.

He asked if I thought Nixon should serve time for what he'd done and I said, well, what did he think? He said, "Yes, sir, and throw the key away." He gave us a booth off in a corner.

Tommy Walt and I talked more about collecting grease from restaurants as we both ate the Tampico Combination Special of two cheese enchiladas, a tamale, a taco, refried beans, rice and a guacamole salad on the side. People who traveled around said there was no better Tex-Mex food south of Chicago, north of Dallas, west of Boston, east of Tucson.

I said to Tommy Walt: "I'm not sure I fully understand this. Let's take here, Chiquita and Ralph's, as a for-instance. How much grease would this place generate?"

"Not much. Mexican food places are medium grease producers. The biggest are hamburger and steak and fried chicken places. The smallest are Italian. Unless they do a lot of veal work."

Veal work?

I did not know how I was going to like having my son talk about the difference in the amount of grease generated by different kinds of restaurants.

"How did you get to know so much about restaurant grease?" I asked.

"A salesman for Procter and Gamble soap told me about it first. I've done a lot of research on my own since."

"You said you could make a good living doing this?"

"Thirty-five thousand a year, minimum."

"Thirty-five thousand. Are you sure, son?"

"Yes, sir."

"That's three times what I make as lieutenant governor of Oklahoma."

"I know."

·2·
Veal Work

Tommy Walt and I left it that night at Chiquita & Ralph's agreeing that I would broach the subject with his mother when she returned in two days from a JackieMart Expansion Safari to Arkansas. He knew leaving JackieMarts Inc. was going to hurt her feelings and he wanted my help in explaining it to her. In the meantime, he would assemble all the specifics and facts needed to launch the grease collection business. Meaning, how much it would cost.

I spent most of the rest of the night turning over in bed and turning over in my head ideas for something else to call it besides the grease collection business. There just had to be another name for it. Something that made it sound more presentable. Something a Rotary Club would accept as a membership category. "Recycling—Food"? "Collector—Droppings"?

I also dreamed of conversations in my future. Like with Buffalo Joe:

"Hey, Mack, what did you say Tommy Walt was up to these days?"

"He goes around to Italian veal-work restaurants in the middle of the night collecting their used grease."

"For God's sake, don't tell the Republicans. Is it legal? How's Jackie taking it? What the hell is veal work? Is it legal?"

It was almost out of my mind after I had been at my office for a while Monday morning. Janice Alice Montgomery, my elderly secretary from Cordell, came in first thing to announce that a young man named Calvin Howell Youngfoot was in the outer office. Calvin Howell Youngfoot? She said he claimed to have talked to me after the Oklahoma Southeastern commencement and I had invited him to come by whenever he was in Oklahoma City.

I still drew a blank. I told people all the time to come by my office whenever they were in Oklahoma City. Few of them ever did but I didn't mind those few who did. If you can't come by and say hello to your lieutenant governor, then what's the point of paying taxes and being a Democrat in Oklahoma?

I wasn't busy. I was reading a long story in some eastern magazine named after the Atlantic Ocean about the early political days of Lyndon Johnson. Luther Wallace, the speaker of the house, who was a friend and a smart man who had gone to college in Massachusetts, gave me a Xeroxed copy. He said that for Oklahoma politicians like us, knowing all about LBJ was like a Chevy mechanic knowing everything about an Impala carburetor. Joe had always said Luther was too smart and too honest to make it, and for a while that was true. But we had just gone through two speakers in three years, one through death in a car accident on I-40 east of Henryetta, the other through resignation after it came out that he had hired somebody else to take his Oklahoma bar exam years before. So the legislature, in desperation for somebody smart and honest, turned to Luther. I liked him very much, even if he did give me things like the LBJ article to read.

Calvin Howell Youngfoot came in and sat down across from me. Oh, yeah. Him. What was it he had said to me? I vaguely remembered from Saturday that he had been terribly well dressed for a fresh college graduate. He still was. His pitch-black hair was still perfectly trimmed and combed. I was not good at picking out Choctaws from Cherokees, but clearly he still had the dark skin of an Oklahoma Indian. Probably still Choctaw.

"Thank you so much for seeing me, sir," he said. There was still not much Oklahoma in his voice. I wondered where he had gone to learn to talk that way. I was tempted to ask him if he read a magazine named after the Atlantic Ocean.

"All of the doors in this building are open doors for all citizens," I said. It was a line I had borrowed from an old county commissioner in Adabel, whom I had defeated in my first political race. Buffalo Joe had a better one: "Look into the eyes of all voters and imagine you see your paycheck, Mack. It helps the concentration."

Now I remembered what the young Choctaw had told me Saturday about not being able to get a job as a spy, and I sighed. He brought it up immediately.

"To be an intelligence agent has been my dream since I

was a little boy," said Calvin Howell Youngfoot. "I want to take risks for my country just like you said in your commencement address, but the government will not let me. I assure you, sir, that I am as qualified as anyone could be to do such work."

There was nothing to do but hear him out. I settled in. I listened while he told in minute detail about first talking to a CIA recruiter who'd come to his campus, and then filling out a massive background application. He had to put down the address of every house he had ever lived in. Names of neighbors. Schools. Names of teachers and principals. Jobs. Grades. Extracurricular activities. Where had he gone on vacation? Where had he stayed? What languages could he speak, and how well? Names of any overseas family or friends. Interests. Church affiliation and beliefs. Complete family history as far back as grandparents. Details on mother and father. Their occupations, education and interests. Was he related to anybody in government? Did he know anybody in government? Had he ever been arrested? For what? When, where? Disposition? Had he ever used drugs? When, where, what? What were his hobbies? Did he drive a car? Did he have a pilot's license? Had he been a Boy Scout? A Cub Scout? What members of his family from grandfathers on—including uncles and cousins—had served in the U.S. military? In anybody else's military? What books had he read over the past twelve months? What magazines and newspapers did he read regularly? Occasionally? Afraid of heights? High rates of speed? Describe his proficiency with firearms, explosives, hand-to-hand combat, electronics and sports, if any.

He said next came a four-hour interview with a CIA

representative in an Oklahoma City hotel room. Every detail on that application was gone over. Then a few weeks later he was summoned to Washington for a lie detector test and several other interviews, including two with psychiatrists. The only thing that turned up on the lie detector, he said, was a long-forgotten time he had stolen a hubcap off a Ford Mercury in a Piggly Wiggly parking lot.

It was some story. I had completely changed my opinion of him by the time he had finished.

"I passed everything, I am sure, sir," he said finally. "There was absolutely nothing negative that could possibly have turned up because there is nothing like that to turn up."

He was clearly impressed with himself. That was fine. He should have been. I was impressed with him but also with what he meant about the quality of students we were turning out at our small Oklahoma state universities. There was a great tendency around Oklahoma City to think of the University of Oklahoma at Norman and Oklahoma State at Stillwater as the only two colleges in Oklahoma that mattered.

"If I may speak frankly for a minute, sir," he said. "I think they turned me down because I have the dark skin of an Indian. I think they think I am not smart enough to be one of their spies."

That did it. I knew what being discriminated against was all about. All one-eyed people do. There were several times in my life, particularly when I was young, that having only one eye was held against me. I suddenly very much wanted this young man to fulfill his dream. So right then and there I decided to help him. It was a terrible decision, among the

most terrible of my career in public service. And even with
the ability to look back in light of everything, I still cannot
explain it fully. Sure, he was a nice young Oklahoman in
need and I was the nice lieutenant governor who liked to
help people in need because I didn't have much else to do.
But I wasn't running an employment agency. He was not
my responsibility just because I had delivered his class's
commencement address. I had no obligation to do anything.
Besides, what in the world did I think I could do to influence
decisions at the Central Intelligence Agency in Washington,
D.C., a mysterious outfit of spies about which the most I
knew was that it had botched an invasion of Cuba?

My words to him haunt me to this day. I said: "I stand
ready to do whatever I can to help. I have no idea what it
could be, though. I have no clout, pull or even any contacts
with the CIA or anything like that. I doubt if I could even
get through to anybody up there on the phone."

The nice young Youngfoot's face lit up. He clearly had
an idea.

"I must find a way to demonstrate my abilities. If the
CIA could only see what I could do, then I know they would
hire me, Indian, dark skin and all."

"I don't know, but I wouldn't think they would take
people on for tryouts."

"My college career counselor told me about a young man
who wanted to be a salesman for IBM, but they wouldn't
hire him. He went out on his own and sold five companies
on buying IBM computers and then took the orders to IBM.
They hired him on the spot and he's now a regional vice-
president in Minneapolis. What if I uncovered a Russian spy
here in Oklahoma and turned him over to the CIA?"

I leaned across my desk and lowered my voice. "Do you know of any Russian spies in Oklahoma?"

"No, sir. But there must be some. The Russians have them all over the United States, I hear. My reading adds up that way, at least."

"What is there to spy on in Oklahoma?"

He shrugged.

I told Calvin Howell Youngfoot that I would give his dilemma some thought and attention. But I would not be optimistic about my turning up anything. I asked him to leave his phone number with Janice Alice Montgomery on his way out. I also told him I would find somebody to give him a tour of the capitol building if he was interested.

He wasn't. He thanked me profusely for everything and got up to leave.

"Sir, didn't I read in *The Daily Oklahoman* or somewhere that you were a close friend of Director Hayes of the Oklahoma Bureau of Investigation?" he said at the office door.

"That's right," I replied. "He's a great friend of mine and of every Oklahoman."

C. Harold Hayes and I were a match. The joke around the capitol was that it was our mutual deformities that made us friends. Who else but a one-eared OBI director could a one-eyed lieutenant governor have as his best friend, anyhow? And vice versa. I had lost my eye in a kick-the-can game back in Kansas; C. had lost his ear in an accident on a police pistol range. Our match had mostly to do with trust and talk. For some reason the first time we really had any business together we found that we could each depend on the other. The business was a crazy thing involving a national TV reporter and a story about an underworld organization called the Okies that operated out of Oklahoma. From the beginning C. said it was a crock and with the help of others we headed off what could have been a terrible problem for the Sooner State. Since then we had seen each other at least a few times a month for lunch in the backseat of his car or in my office and around the capitol. We liked to talk to each other. About the idiots we came across in our daily lives, the news, baseball, thunderstorms and other things that mattered to each of us.

"I'll bet he'd know about any Russian spies in Oklahoma," the young Choctaw said.

I smiled. He left.

And I resumed my reading about the Texas boyhood of Lyndon Baines Johnson.

Less than an hour later Janice Alice buzzed me to say C. was on line 2835 returning my call.

"Yes, sir, Mr. One-Eyed Lieutenant Governor?" he said. "I am your servant."

"I didn't call you, Mr. One-Eared OBI Director," I said, and it was the truth.

"Somebody called here a while ago and said you were looking for me. I have the note right here on one of those little pink slips in front of me."

"Wrong. It didn't happen."

"Well, what a disappointment. To be looked for by the lieutenant governor of Oklahoma is an honor and a pleasure."

Something then did occur to me. I said: "Look, as long as I have you, I do have a question."

"Shoot."

"Are there any Russian spies in Oklahoma?"

"Well . . . yes and no," he said, his voice dropping noticeably on the other end of the phone.

"How can that be?"

"Why are you asking, Mack?"

"I am trying to help out a young Oklahoman who needs one."

"Needs one what?"

"One Russian spy."

"A young Oklahoman who needs one Russian spy? Are you drunk, Mack?"

"He wants to be a CIA man himself. . . ."

"Don't say any more on an open line. How about lunch?"

"Burger King or McDonald's?"

"Your call, sir. I'll be by at twelve thirty-two precisely."

C., which he always said stood for Cool, had very strange habits. Like lunch. He ate the same thing every day. A hamburger all the way except onions, an order of fries and a chocolate milk shake. Every day. Every working day, at least. The only variance was whether the hamburger was a Big Mac from McDonald's or a Whopper from Burger King. He also did not like to go inside to sit down. He much preferred eating in the car. If somebody was with him, as I was this day and an average of three or four days a month, he sat in the backseat of his black armored Lincoln Continental OBI director's car with his guest. Like on a picnic. Like it was a big deal.

I chose Burger King this time. We went to the one just north of the capitol on Lincoln Boulevard. One of his young agents drove us around as we ate. And talked. I told him about young Calvin Howell Youngfoot.

"So your theory is that if you can help him find a Russian spy to turn in to the CIA, they'll say, 'Well, lookie there at how good he is,' and hire him?"

"That's the theory."

"It's a stupid theory, Mack. A very stupid theory."

I said: "What if some smart young man came into your office with a John Dillinger–type bank robber under his arm? Wouldn't you hire him for the OBI?"

"No, sir. I'd say, 'Thank you, Mr. Smart Young Man.' I'd very quickly put cuffs and irons on the Dillinger type and I'd advise the kid to get help for his mental problem. People who go around arresting John Dillinger types on their own have serious mental problems."

We talked about a few other things. And I told him about Tommy Walt's going into the restaurant grease collection business.

He said: "I hope he knows that's one rough business. Fierce, mean competition. Local PDs have to break up fights all the time among them."

It was something I did not want to know any more about. I brought it back to Calvin Howell Youngfoot, Smart Young Man.

"What did you mean, 'yes and no,' about there being any Russian spies in Oklahoma?" I asked.

"Just that. Yes and no. In one way there is a Russian spy in Oklahoma but in another way there isn't. It depends on how you look at it. The CIA and the FBI already know all about it, so it wouldn't help your bright young Indian anyhow."

"Know all about what?"

"I can't say any more."

"Why not?"

31

"Top secret."

He changed the subject to marshmallows. He was planning to have his two grandsons, ages eight and eleven, over for the weekend and he wanted to toast marshmallows in the backyard. But he had never gotten the full hang of how to roast them without burning them. How can you tell when they are perfectly done? What's the secret, Mack? he asked. I told him if there was a secret it had escaped me too. I had the same problem he did with marshmallows. Cook them hot dogs instead, I suggested. I am, he said. I wanted to do both. Buy them ice cream for dessert, I said. Forget marshmallows. Kids these days don't like them that much anyhow. He said that was because their parents and grandparents hadn't passed on their love of marshmallows properly.

I brought it back to the Russian spy in Oklahoma.

"I can keep secrets, C. You know that. Tell me about the Russian spy."

He was twirling his straw around the bottom of his milk shake cup. The fries and the Whopper were gone. We were entering the west parking lot at the capitol, where he was going to drop me off.

"All right," he said. "I'll tell you just this. There is a Russian spy in Oklahoma but he no longer spies. That's all I'm saying."

"He no longer spies?"

"That's what I said. I'm not saying another thing."

"You mean Oklahoma is a kind of Sunset Retirement Living Center for a Russian spy?"

"Leave it alone, Mack."

"I am the lieutenant governor of Oklahoma. I have a right to know such things."

We were stopped now at the west entrance to the capitol.

"Leave it alone, Mack. I shouldn't have said a thing."

"I am the lieutenant governor...."

"Yes, sir. Now will you get out of this car and get on with being it."

I thanked him for lunch and got out of the car.

There is a Russian spy in Oklahoma but he no longner spies?

Leave it alone, Mack.

Oh, how I wish I had.

Sometimes it seemed as if I spent half my on-job time as lieutenant governor attending funerals of prominent Sooner citizens. I had three funerals that afternoon. First, a Jewish synagogue service in Guthrie for a sixty-two-year-old heart attack victim who was a fourth-generation candy maker. His company made the famous Guthrie Nutget, a deliciously chewy goo of caramel and cashew nuts covered with thick milk chocolate. Then came a small Southern Baptist funeral for the 1956 Oklahoma Farmer of the Year who passed away in a Spencer nursing home at the age of eighty-two. And finally, a huge Episcopal service in Nichols Hills for Johnny Hank (Fats) Ragsdale, a delightful guy who once served state prison time at McAlester for fraud and gambling but went on to become highly successful and respectable. After paying his debt to society he founded SSO, Sooner State Optical, which operated hundreds of optical stores all over the state that promised to examine your eyes and have glasses made and in your hands within fifty-nine minutes or it was all free. The policy was called The 59 Promise. He was seventy-one years old and died of unspecified natural causes. They called him Fats because he weighed 315 pounds; he was the smartest card player in Oklahoma.

What I had on my agenda for the evening was to talk to Tommy Walt's lovely mother about her son's desire to quit his job with her to collect grease from restaurants.

I met Jackie for dinner at Faulkenberry's, the finest steak house in Oklahoma City. She wanted to go home for something light after her Arkansas trip but I insisted on Faulkenberry's. We have something to talk about that must be talked about at Faulkenberry's, I said.

Jackie was the smartest woman in Oklahoma. Buffalo Joe and C. kidded me all the time about how I married over my head and out of my smarts. Buffalo Joe, who was married to one of the dumbest women in Oklahoma, said once: "Living with Jackie must be what keeps you so humble and nice, Mack." Meaning, among other things, I guess, that he did not live with such a woman, so that explained why he wasn't humble and nice like me.

Jackie was also gorgeous. Short blond hair, sparkling blue eyes, beige silk skin, tight fashion-magazine figure, a smile that melted cast iron. She came into Faulkenberry's like a princess, like a homecoming queen, like she owned the only chain of drive-thru grocery stores in Oklahoma. Like she owned Oklahoma.

She told me first about her Expansion Safari.

"They're different over there, Mack," she said of Arkansas. "We talked to a banker in Arkadelphia who insisted on taking us and a stopwatch to a Piggly Wiggly, then to a 7-Eleven, to a Safeway, to a Burger King and to several other places to time how long it took to buy things. He wrote down all of the times on a yellow legal pad and then said,

Very interesting. Very interesting in what way? I asked. Very interesting in that it does not prove anything. So? I said. So, it comes down to your word on whether JackieMarts can get groceries and other merchandise to people quicker than others can. I said that was not the only point of JackieMarts. Another point was that people didn't have to get out of their cars to shop. He said he wasn't sure the people of Arkadelphia, Arkansas, minded getting out of their cars that much. Well, if that's the case, then Arkadelphia is probably not the place for a JackieMart. He said he would investigate the matter further and decide within a few days if he would loan the money to the young Vietnamese man who wanted to open a JackieMart franchise there. He talked like he was deciding whether to merge Oklahoma and Arkansas into one state. Heaven forbid. I find it amazing how a place like Arkansas can be so close and yet so far away."

She always liked my funeral stories, so I told her about the three of the day. Fats Ragsdale's was the most elaborate and interesting. His widow had hired the Central Oklahoma Lutheran College glee club, The Messengers, and the Enid Philharmonic Orchestra to perform Fats's favorite music. Unfortunately, some of his favorites were not religious in nature and that seemed to offend some of the blue-haired women and blue-nosed men in attendance. I had to admit, "Poor Jud" and "On the Street Where You Live" did seem a bit out of place at an Episcopal funeral.

Jackie said the high point of her three days in Arkansas was the wedding in Hopeville of the young Vietnamese man who was in line to open the first JackieMart franchise in Arkansas, the good banker permitting. The ceremony was in a small café where the bride worked as a waitress. It was a one-rose ceremony, the groom giving the bride a single red rose as a symbol of their love. The reception was also in the café. They served coconut pie, coffee and milk. There was no music except for a few songs played on the jukebox during the reception. The café was closed for business during the wedding but many of the guests were regular customers. The bride and groom were given a honeymoon trip—two nights free at the Days Inn motel in Pine Bluff—as a wedding present by the employees of the local IGA food store, where the groom worked as the assistant night manager.

"It sounds silly but it wasn't," said Jackie. "It was the most moving wedding I have ever been to. All weddings should be held out in the real world somewhere. Drugstores, dime stores, car washes, cafés . . ."

"Speaking of cafés . . ." I said quickly. I had my opening. The big moment had come. "Do you know how much grease a restaurant like Faulkenberry's here generates?"

"No," she replied. Like I had just asked her to name the first fourteen presidents of the United States.

"Lots. More than any other kind of restaurant, because this is a steak house. Tex-Mex places don't create that much. Neither do doughnut shops, strangely enough, because most of the grease they use is absorbed right into the doughnuts. Italian places don't either unless they do a lot of veal work."

"Veal work? Mack, what's wrong?" Her face turned a lighter beige. She reached across the table and grabbed my right hand. "Are you sick? Has something happened? Mack, what's wrong? Have you had a breakdown?"

"No, nothing's wrong with me. I am completely normal. . . ."

"Is it that idiot Joe Hayman? What crazy, stupid, idiotic,

imbecilic, nonsensical, indictable offense has he committed now? That man should be locked up. How he ever got to be governor of this fine state is more than I will ever figure out. You should run against him. Yes, that's it. Run against him next time, Mack. He's crazy. He's done this to you. He's driven you crazy too. Here you are, talking about grease being absorbed into doughnuts and Italian restaurants doing veal work. It's his fault. Your friend C. is right in calling him Buffalo Chip. That's exactly what he is. . . ."

"Joe has nothing to do with this. Tommy Walt is who has to do with this."

Now she really jerked those blue eyes big. "What's he done? Is he in trouble? Is he hurt?"

"He wants to go into the restaurant grease collection business."

The color returned to her face. Her eyes went back to their normal size. She laughed. "Now *that* is crazy. What a relief. I thought it was something serious."

"He is serious."

"Impossible. Get out of the drive-thru grocery business? Impossible."

I told her about his desire to be on his own.

"It would be different if it was his father's instead of his mother's business, wouldn't it, Mack? Tell me the truth. He's embarrassed to be in business with his mother, isn't he? I thought he would never let something like that bother him. . . ."

"That's not it. I am sure of that. I really am."

I talked as quickly and persuasively as I could to make her believe that. Tommy Walt really was a better, stronger man than that. I honestly did not believe he was embarrassed to be working for his mother and I did not think it had one thing to do with what he wanted to do.

Jackie finally seemed convinced too, and it came back to the other part. The restaurant grease collection business.

"I can't think of any worse way to make a living," she said quietly. "How do they collect it, anyway?"

"In barrels."

"Barrels? Whose barrels?"

"His. He'd have to buy some barrels."

"When would he go around with his barrels?" She shuddered at the thought.

"At night after the restaurants close."

Jackie was not an indiscriminate crier. She cried only when it was logical and normal to cry. Now she put a Faulkenberry's white linen napkin to her eyes. Tears were forming.

"Where did we go wrong, Mack?" she asked.

"I don't know," I replied.

·3·
Start-Up Costs

BUFFALO JOE had a great surprise for me the next morning. His best surprise. He was going to be leaving the state for a while and I would step in as acting governor during his absence.

I loved being acting governor of Oklahoma.

Governor Ralph Joseph Hayman was called Buffalo Joe by some because he was from Buffalo, Oklahoma, and by others because he resembled a buffalo in physical appearance. C. was one of a few who called him Buffalo Chip, as in "dung." Jackie and C. and a lot of Sooner citizens, Democrats and others, didn't care much for Buffalo Joe. And, sure, he sometimes made it difficult to care for him. He thought highly of himself, more highly than he did of anyone else. He was full of those wise sayings of his, called Joeisms by the capitol press. He spoke mostly with the "we" pronoun.

He repeated himself a lot. He was an absolutely pure paranoiac. But he was wonderful to me, calling me the Second Man of Oklahoma and treating me in a way that made me think he really meant it. I figured his being governor was a matter between him and the people of Oklahoma, just like my being lieutenant governor. Meanwhile, he was the First Man of Oklahoma and I was there to serve him and the people who elected us both. He was also great entertainment.

We were sitting side by side on an outdoor speakers' platform in front of the National Cowboy Hall of Fame. A collection of western TV series was being given to the museum, which was north of the capitol in Oklahoma City, on Northeast 63rd Street. We were both there at the ceremony to add the full weight of state government to the thank you the Hollywood donors had already received from the museum. I was keen on the collection because it included a copy of every TV show made by my all-time favorite, Roy Rogers. I had actually met Roy and Dale Evans, Gabby Hayes and Trigger when they were making a movie in Adabel many years before, but my admiration for Roy went back to listening to him on KFH radio from Wichita, Kansas.

"You're going to be the governor again, the governor again," Joe said while the Oklahoma State University Cowboy Band played the themes from *Gunsmoke, Have Gun, Will Travel, Bonanza, Wanted: Dead or Live, The Rifleman* and *Maverick*.

He told me he was going to Japan on what he called a shopping trip for Oklahoma as part of the state's "Business Is OK in Oklahoma" program. He would be talking with government and business leaders about doing business with

· Duncan Manor ·
SONGWRITER SERIES

elliot sedgwick	10.1.2016
the deep hollow	11.5.2016
rebecca rego	12.3.2016
dan hubbard	1.7.2017
stone & snow	2.4.2017
nick africano	3.4.2017
chicago farmer	4.1.2017

LIMITED TICKETS AVAILABLE!

TOUR THE MANOR

· ALL SHOWS START AT 7:00PM ·

· INTIMATE HOUSE CONCERTS BENEFITTING THE RESTORATION OF Duncan Manor, A 501(c)3 NOT-FOR-PROFIT ORGANIZATION ·

· $30 ADVANCE TICKETS ONLY AT www.WRDUNCANMANOR.COM ·

Duncan Manor

· PRESENTS ·

SPIRITS OF THE PAST

A HAUNTED HISTORY TOUR

featuring!

Community Players THEATRE

October 14 + 15th, 2016

LEARN ABOUT THE HISTORY OF THIS LOCAL LANDMARK!

ARTWORK BY MISS CHRIS   LIVE MUSIC BY CHICKEN SHACK   FOOD BY HEALTHY IN A HURRY SPARKYS BBQ

TOURS RUN 6-11PM & RESERVATIONS ARE REQUIRED
VISIT WWW.WRDUNCANMANOR.COM FOR RESERVATIONS

· BENEFITTING THE RESTORATION OF _Duncan Manor_, A 501(C)3 NOT-FOR-PROFIT ORGANIZATION ·

and in Oklahoma. He was also going to attend a national governors' conference in California on the way out of the country. So he would be out of the state and I would be acting governor of Oklahoma for eleven days.

I told him I would do my best to keep the ship of state on an even keel in his absence.

"We trust you not to do anything crazy, Mack," he said. "We trust you." He said it twice. For emphasis.

Joe winked at me, as he often did when we talked about my being acting governor when he was out of the state. The wink meant that we both knew one day he would be moving on to be president or vice-president of the United States and it would be a natural for me to replace him as the permanent governor of Oklahoma.

This would be the fourth time I had served as acting governor. But none of the other stints had been for more than five or six days. Eleven days was a long time.

And as the band and the speakers played on about TV westerns, I thought about all the people around who would have ideas about what I should do during those eleven days. Like appoint them or their brother-in-law to the state pardon-and-parole board. Like call the legislature into special session and pass a special bill that would pay for the construction of a new international airport in Adabel. Like order the state highway department to resurface all roads in Kingman County. Like change the color of the state flag from light blue to green. Like fire the state industrial development board. Like disband the all–white male state supreme court and replace it with five Indian and/or black members. Like declare war on Texas. Like invade Arkansas.

I loved being acting governor of Oklahoma.

* * *

The first person I told was C. I ran into him in the hallway outside the senate chamber right after I returned to the capitol. He was in the building for a legislative budget hearing, his annual trip to the hearing table to say crime was up again in Oklahoma and that meant the OBI budget needed to go up again to fight off the drug dealers, murderers, bandits, con men and others who were jeopardizing the peace and tranquility of our Sooner State. The OBI budget was the only branch of state government besides the highway department that always got an increase with no or few questions asked. No member of the legislature wanted to appear soft on crime or opposed to building highways.

C. was delighted about Buffalo Joe's plans to leave the state with me in charge. "Hallelujah," he said. "Call out the National Guard and seal off the borders so he can't come back."

He said a senator had just asked him if the OBI wanted the legislature to provide funds to buy a couple of helicopter gunships like those used in Vietnam.

"Can you imagine it, Mack? Agents of the Oklahoma Bureau of Investigation swooping down across Turner Turnpike wasting speeding truckers and cigarette smugglers with rockets from helicopters. Wow, wow. Hot stuff. I wish somebody would pass a law prohibiting members of the legislature from watching television."

Then I said: "Did you tell the committee about the Russian spy who doesn't spy anymore?"

C. grabbed me and almost threw me against a wall. "Hush," he said. "Hush."

He took me by the arm as if I were under arrest and led me back to my office and closed the door.

"Mack, I told you that was top secret. Top secret means nobody knows. Top secret means I should not have told even you."

"I am the lieutenant governor of this state, soon to become the acting governor."

"Oh, my, yes. Oh, my, yes. But you were given that information in your capacity as the friend of a stupid idiot who can't keep his mouth shut. It was unofficial. Colley would kill me if he knew I told you anything."

"Colley? Who's Colley?"

"The guy who will kill me if he ever finds out I told you—or anyone else," he said, as if he believed this Colley might very well do it.

"Look, how can there be a Russian spy in Oklahoma and you not do anything about it?"

"I told you. He doesn't spy anymore."

"How do you know that? They said Fats Ragsdale gave up gambling, but I never believed it."

"He didn't. He just quit it in Oklahoma. Leave it alone, Mack. Please. Promise me you will leave it alone. Promise. This is serious business."

"Sure."

Sure. Well, maybe sure. It would be hard and unnatural to leave it alone. This kind of thing had a way of burning empty holes in my mind that needed filling with all there was to know.

He hadn't been gone fifteen minutes when Janice Alice buzzed me to say young Calvin Howell Youngfoot was on the phone. Just checking in to see if there were any developments.

"Tell him I'm on the trail of one," I said.

I said it without really thinking.

Then Janice Alice reminded me that I was due at Hunan Westend in five minutes.

It was over lunch at Hunan Westend that Jackie, good mother and great woman, gave her final official blessing to Tommy Walt and his restaurant grease plans. They had been talking about it all morning in their offices at JackieMart headquarters. They agreed that it was not what Jackie would have chosen but, after all, it was Tommy Walt's life, not hers. Tommy Walt thanked me profusely later for having paved the way for him. "I could never have done it without you, Dad," he said.

Now came Tommy Walt to the celebration lunch with a stack of papers and enthusiasm for getting on with it. And that brought it down to what I thought was going to be the hard part. Money.

He gave Jackie and me each a copy of his equipment list: A leased pickup truck with a tailgate lift. Twenty tin barrels. A hand truck for moving the barrels of grease from restaurant kitchens out to alleys. A drum pump and metal funnels to get the grease in the barrels in the first place. A hose with a nozzle to clean the barrels after the liquid grease was delivered to the rendering plant. Coveralls and heavy gloves for him and an employee. An answering machine, an adding machine, a typewriter and various paper invoices and stationery for the office.

Then he gave us another list, of start-up costs. There was rent for a small warehouse/garage/office. Insurance. Telephone and other utilities deposits. Gasoline for the truck. Licenses and permits.

He had numbers written out to the right of each item. I looked down at the bottom to a total: $1,875.

I said: "This figure here, the total is, I take it, what you want from us?"

"No, sir. I just wanted you to know what was involved."

Said Jackie: "Your father and I would be delighted to get you started."

"No, Mom. I'm going to borrow the money from a bank. It has to be my deal all the way or it won't work."

I said: "All right, then. I'll call Jack Delaware at Oklahoma Bank and Trust. . . ."

"A guy at South Canadian Bank and Trust is already set to get me going," said Tommy Walt.

Jackie and I exchanged a matched set of proud smiles. Tommy Walt, our only son, was going to be just fine.

There remained only one problem.

"Have you thought about what to call your company and its business?" I said.

"I was thinking of something like Boomer Sooner Grease Collection Service. Or I might make it personal like Mom does. Call it Tommy Walt's or maybe use my initials. Do you have any suggestions?"

"Is there any other name for what you'll be doing? Anything other than 'grease collection service'? Something about 'recycling Oklahoma' or the like?"

He smiled. "I'm open to all suggestions, sir."

"I'm thinking."

Then Jackie asked: "Aren't you liable to get a lot of grease in your hair and on your skin and around?"

"Yes, ma'am. But there are good, strong soaps that will wash it right off."

"Good," she replied.

"Do you have any restaurants lined up yet?" I asked.

"No, sir. I'm going to make my first calls this afternoon. I have appointments with five fried chicken places."

I looked around Hunan Westend. "How about starting right here right now?"

"Chinese restaurants are near-zero generators of grease," he said, all business. "Worse even than Tex-Mex."

"Too bad they're not into veal work," I said.

Tommy Walt insisted on picking up the tab for lunch. And eventually the three of us walked out together to the parking lot. He to his Pontiac Trans Am to pay his first call on a nearby Kentucky Fried Chicken place. Jackie to her white Cadillac Eldorado to return to JackieMart headquarters. And me to my blue Buick Skylark to resume my duties as Second Man of Oklahoma.

·4·
Ask Jackie

C. KNEW WHAT I was up to from the very beginning. I had called him and said I had done some checking around for a solution to his problem and thought I might have something. What problem? he asked. The marshmallow problem, I replied.

We worked it out that he would drop by my house just before seven.

Now it was seven and he was there. I took him into the den for a brief diversionary move. I showed him old Denco Bus Lines and Turner Transportation Company bus depot signs I had tacked up on the wall. I had always had a special interest in intercity buses, going back to when I was growing up in Kansas, so occasionally as I moved around I would pick up old items from old companies. Just to have them. I particularly liked the little metal signs that hung in front of drugstores and service stations where the buses stopped in small towns. People collect railroad things, so why not bus stuff?

We moved out onto the patio, and I went through a whole little routine. Lighting up some charcoal in the barbecue on the patio. Putting some marshmallows on the end of wire clothes hangers that I carefully undid and extended. Sticking the end of the hangers a half-inch into the marshmallows. Mouthing on and on about how the fire must be just right, the marshmallow must be held just six inches from the fire.

"Drop the marshmallow act, Mack," he said finally. "I am not going to tell you one more thing about that Russian spy. I told you to drop it. Now drop it."

"I can't."

"Why not? Good God. It can't be just because some Indian kid wants to grow up and work for the CIA."

"It's a mystery, C. I love mysteries. You know that. There's something overwhelmingly exciting to think that there is a Russian spy in Oklahoma who doesn't spy anymore. I want to know about him. That's all. I can't help it."

"Hey, Mack. This stuff is too important to go play mystery with. If you want to play games, go ask Jackie. That's it."

"Yes, sir."

C. shook my hand and headed for his car.

"Hey, you don't have to leave just like that. Have something to drink."

"I have to go. Don't press me any more on this. Ask Jackie. Not me. That's it. Forget it."

* * *

48

It was more than a half-hour later that it dawned on me C. might have been saying something after all. "Ask Jackie. Not me. That's it." Maybe.

She wasn't home. She had called me at the capitol at five to say she was going to have to spend part of the evening with a delegation from Paragould, Arkansas. She and her Expansion Safari team had decided definitely to put four JackieMarts in Paragould, but there were three separate investor groups competing to come in as partner/operators or franchisees. The three had been selected out of an original list of twelve applicants. Now one of the three finalists had asked to make a case again before a decision was made. The meeting would be at JackieMart headquarters on May Avenue, out by the state fairgrounds. She would be home by nine.

She told me all this on the phone. The smart and obvious thing for me to do was wait a couple of hours until she came home and then ask her about the Russian spy. Obviously, whatever she knew about a Russian spy in Oklahoma would keep until then. And that was my decision. I would wait.

Obviously.

I roasted four marshmallows and ate them. Then I put on a hot dog, stuck it with some mustard between a folded piece of white Wonder bread and ate it. I noticed for the first time in my life that a lot of grease dripped out of hot dogs onto the hot coals. I wondered for the first time in my life how it might be collected and saved. I wondered if that would be the next phase for Tommy Walt. Asking ordinary Sooner citizens to save their ordinary Sooner grease for collection and sale to rendering plants.

49

All that took only fifteen minutes. I drank some gulps from a can of Dr Pepper. It was still an hour and a half before Jackie would be home.

So I poured the rest of the Dr Pepper on the hot charcoal and sped away in my blue Buick Skylark for JackieMart headquarters.

The headquarters were in a building that had once been a taxi garage. Jackie had bought it from Checker when it merged with Yellow and Blue Top and moved all its operations into Yellow's facility across from the old farmers' market. Yellow had bought that place from Oklahoma Blue Arrow Motorcoaches, Tommy Walt's old employer, when it built a new garage and office farther west on Interstate 55. Jackie used two-thirds of her building as a warehouse. Here she kept boxes of canned goods, paper products like TP and Kleenex, toothpaste and other nonperishable stuff for distribution to her stores. Huge red-white-and-blue tractor trailers with her face painted on both sides went out every morning from headquarters to JackieMarts throughout Oklahoma. The rest was for offices. Hers and those of her administrative and supervisory personnel.

She had come a long way from the first JackieMart in west Oklahoma City. It started with her simple genius idea that there ought to be a place the harassed young mother, hurried young father, elderly grandparent, single drunk or whoever could go to buy bread, milk and other basic convenience-store items without having to get out of the car. Her JackieMarts were set up like McDonald's and Burger King drive-thrus. Customers drove to an order station, spoke their orders into a microphone and then drove around to a pick-up station. The trick and the challenge was to have the merchandise arranged and organized in such a way that it could be gathered and sacked in the few precious seconds from ordering to picking up. To stand inside a JackieMart at a busy time was to watch a miracle of coordination, talent and speed.

When people walked through the front door of the head-quarters, the first thing they saw was a huge multicolored map of Oklahoma with three-inch-high pictures of Jackie's face, the corporate logo, pinned to each JackieMart location. Four were in Oklahoma City. Two in Tulsa and Muskogee. And one each in Lawton, Ponca City, Pauls Valley, Ard-more, McAlester, Blackwell, Hugotown, Tonkawa, Adabel and Utoka.

As I glanced at the map now, I wondered what they were going to do with Paragould and Arkadelphia. They were in Arkansas, not Oklahoma.

There was a sound of voices coming from the conference room, which I knew to be just off the reception area. I headed for it.

I stuck my head inside. The talking stopped. Jackie said, "Hi, Mack. This is a surprise. Gentlemen, this is my husband, the lieutenant governor of Oklahoma."

There were four good men of Paragould in the room, two of them of Oriental extraction. All were impressed, I could tell, that the lieutenant governor of Oklahoma had just happened by. I went around and shook their hands, said my name, welcomed them to the Sooner State.

Jackie did not have to be told that I needed to talk to her. In private. Obviously about something important, or I wouldn't have broken into her meeting this way. Obviously. We stepped down the hall to the executive suite and into her private office.

"It's Tommy Walt, isn't it? He's been hurt collecting grease," she said once the door was closed. "No, it's one of the girls...."

We had three daughters. One, Walterene, was Tommy Walt's twin. She was an intensive care nurse in Tulsa; to my mind this was the hardest work there was in the world. Our other two, Stephanie and Cathy, were still in school. And doing well.

I allayed her fears and then said I was interested in locating a Russian spy who was in Oklahoma but who no longer spies.

"I asked C. for a clue but he said he wouldn't give me one," I said. "He said if I wanted to play mystery I should ask Jackie. So I have come to ask Jackie."

Her office was three times larger than mine. And it looked like a picture in a home-and-garden magazine. There were two handsome upholstered chairs in front of her long sleek desk, which had a glass top and silver metal legs. There was a couch and two similar chairs bunched around a glass coffee table against the opposite wall. Everything in there was long and sleek. And modern. There were tall plants, books and silver-framed photographs of me and the kids and her first JackieMart.

We had taken seats next to each other on the couch. She reached over with her right hand and placed it on my forehead.

"You really are coming down with something, Mack. Are you feverish? They say that's an early warning sign that something might be breaking...."

I pressed ahead with a little bit about Calvin Howell Youngfoot and how it all began. And I told her again what C. had said.

"Mack, it was just his way of saying that if you want to play little games, go play them with your wife," she said. "It was not a clue." There was a touch of impatience in her manner. I was sorry to notice. Jackie was not fond of wasting time. And increasingly anything that did not have to do with JackieMarts seemed to her like wasting time.

"I don't know. Like I say, that's all C. said. . . ."

"I am in the drive-thru grocery store business, Mack. I know nothing about Russian spies. Nothing. Now, if it is all right with you, I will get back to resolving the franchisee problem in Paragould, Arkansas."

"Certainly," I said. "What are you going to do about the map out in the lobby?"

"We have Arkansas being made of the same material that will fit right next to Oklahoma there on the wall where it belongs," she said. "I should be home in an hour or two."

"Yes, Madame JackieMart President," I said.

We went out into the hall together.

"Have you heard from Tommy Walt about how he did with his fried chicken places?" she asked.

"Not a thing."

"Congratulations on being acting governor again." I had told her about it in our five-o'clock telephone call.

"Thank you."

"What if you refused to give the job back when he returns?"

I kissed her on the lips and said, "No comment."

* * *

53

Yes, I liked mysteries. I liked tinkering with them, thinking about them, playing with them. Not the kind in books
or on television. The real kind. Such as when State Senator
A suddenly reverses a lifetime position on state employee
pensions. Why did he do it? When Governor B, after threatening publicly to run Representative C out of the Sooner
State, shows up at a small, intimate barbecue in Representative C's backyard. Why? Why did the state highway director suddenly decide to pave a stretch of highway south
of Wilburton? Why does the deputy state auditor keep a
picture of a 1932 Packard sedan on his desk? Why is only
Coke sold in the vending machines on the capitol grounds?
Where's Pepsi? Dr Pepper? And Grapette, my all-time favorite? Why does the face of the early-forties male assistant
librarian turn red whenever in the presence of a late-thirties
female deputy assistant state librarian? And so on. Some
were important, most were not even of interest to anyone
but me. And I was interested only in the process of finding
out. I did not want to know the answers in order to hurt
anybody or use them in any way whatsoever. Although
occasionally something did turn up that I felt was in the
public's interest to be pursued. That's when I usually turned
to C.

No, Buffalo Joe was not keen on my being so curious
about things—particularly things political. His wisdom on
the subject was: "To know the mysteries of politics is like
knowing the mysteries of onions. The mysteries of onions,
Mack. Think about it."

So now I had the mystery of "Ask Jackie." If it was a
real clue, then there were only a couple of answers. Number
one was that Jackie was lying to me. She knew all about a

Russian spy in Oklahoma but simply would not tell me about it. That did not add up. If Jackie knew anything about a Russian spy in Oklahoma it is hard to imagine her not telling me the second she found out. I was the lieutenant governor, for one thing. We had no secrets from each other, for another. So if she knew anything she would have said: "Hey, Mack, guess what? I just found out there is a Russian spy in Oklahoma who doesn't spy anymore. His name is Ivan Stalin and he lives on a farm in Garfield County."

No, Jackie was not holding back anything. Her reaction to my questions had been honest. She did not know a thing. So if "Ask Jackie" meant anything it was something she didn't know she knew. That made sense. What kind of mystery clue would it be if all I had to do was ask Jackie what I asked her? That's if C. had given me a real clue. Which I still did not know for sure.

I decided to give it one last try when she got home. It was after ten and she wanted to go right to bed and to sleep. I wouldn't let her. I had a pot of coffee hot and ready for her in the kitchen. I made her sit down with me at the kitchen table. I made her talk to me.

And in less than five minutes I had the answer to the mystery of the Russian spy in Oklahoma.

"How did the meeting go?" I had said immediately, to warm things up.

"Fine. It went fine," she said. "Once again we have fine candidates for a store. It's going to be a difficult choice as usual. This group is backing a young Korean to be the general manager of all four stores. They say he's a wonderful man who deserves a break."

"Good," I said. "It's great the way you help them out."

I meant it. JackieMarts Inc. had already won plaques from Rotary International and from the Oklahoma International Business Council for hiring and encouraging immigrants and refugees.

"Somebody needs to," she said.

It was at that split second that I figured it out. "How many different kinds of foreigners do you have now?" I asked, trying my best to hold back some heavy breathing.

She answered: "I haven't counted them. Vietnamese, of course. Several Mexicans. Koreans. A Jamaican. Some Cubans. Maybe a few others."

"Any from Europe or places like that?" I said. "Regular white people who look like us?"

"Just one. But he speaks English as well as you or me. Better maybe. He's a handsome, smart man."

"What country's he from?"

"Don't know. Somewhere overseas in Europe."

"What store does he run?"

"The one in Utoka."

If I had had my way I would have zipped off immediately to Utoka. But I had to sit on that for a while because of my duties to my state and my son. Mostly those to my son. I had to go inspect Tommy Walt's place of business.

The address was just south of downtown, east of the Santa Fe tracks. I drove down and around several barely passable mud-tar streets before I found it. It was a one-story red brick building, not more than fifty feet across the front, with an entrance large enough for a car or truck to pass through, now closed by a gray corrugated-tin door. Above the door hung a fresh wooden sign. It was six feet long, two feet high. T.W. GREASE COLLECTORS, it said in sturdy red letters on a white background.

T.W. Grease Collectors.

Tommy Walt, the proud sole proprietor, had asked me to come down to inspect his operation and consult with him on a problem he was having getting it off the ground.

"It may not seem like much, Dad," he said, "but it's all here. I'm ready."

"It's much," I said, shaking his hand and, frankly, holding back a desire to grab him and hug him. The kid had done it.

He explained the smell. The building had been used for years to store spices and flavorings, so now it had the odor of ginger, chili pepper, vanilla and chocolate. He showed me his twenty fifty-gallon tin drums, all neatly arranged on a drum rack. They were clean, ready to go. His truck was a green ten-year-old International Harvester, also clean and ready to go. In the bed of the truck were the proper funnels and pumps and hoses, also clean and ready to go.

Sectioned off from the back wall with thin plywood partitions was a fourteen-foot-square office. Inside, one desk, one telephone, a typewriter and stacks of forms and other paper material were all ready to go.

"Have one," he said, handing me a small calling card. It said, in small black print, "T.W. Grease Collectors. Fast, dependable service." There was a phone number and the address.

"Impressive, son," I said. "This is impressive." I meant it. I stuck the card in a pocket of my suit coat.

He was dressed in a set of brand-new blue-and-white-striped coveralls. They seemed at least a size too big. Most things seemed at least a size too big for Tommy Walt because he was only five-six and skinny. Another set of coveralls lay folded on the desk.

He pointed to the coveralls. "There you see my problem, Dad," he said. "I can't find the right person to fill them. And time is running out. My first pick-up appointment is tomorrow night at a Kentucky Fried Chicken on South Western."

"Where have you looked?"

"Everywhere. I have interviewed more than twenty guys. A few might have worked out, but once I explained in detail the kind of work it was and the hours, they begged off. None of those willing measures up. None of them has the spirit and drive I'm going to need to make a go of this. I can only hire one employee right now, so he has to be right."

"Well, now, that *is* a serious problem...."

"I was wondering if you knew of somebody around the capitol who might be interested. Maybe somebody who is looking for a drastic change from a humdrum life in government?"

"Good idea," I lied. "I'll check around."

It was a terrible idea. Imagine it.

Hi, Mr. Assistant Deputy State Finance and Taxation Director. How would you like to escape from this humdrum life and go around in the middle of the night collecting old restaurant grease? There is an opportunity for you just for the asking. Call this number and ask for T.W. Tell him the lieutenant governor of Oklahoma sent you.

I had no idea what I could do, but I promised to do what I could as quickly as I could, and we said our good-byes.

Calvin Howell Youngfoot. Mr. Eager Slick Young Man. There he was, waiting for me, when I arrived back at the capitol. He was standing next to the little black-lettering-on-blue LIEUTENANT GOVERNOR sign by my reserved parking space. I wanted to turn the other way, to wave him off and away.

"Good afternoon, sir," he said after I got out of the car. "I don't mean to make a nuisance of myself, but I could not help but wonder if you had turned up anything about a spy. Your secretary said you were on the trail of one?"

"Yeah, but I don't think it's working out." I figured the less said, the better. "Maybe it's time you considered a different career. How about the highway department?"

"The what, sir?"

"What if I call the head of the state highway department and get you a job interview? They are always on the lookout for bright young men to assist their district engineers around the state. Building roads and bridges is the number-one growth industry in our state. Good future, good prospects."

His handsome dark face crinkled. "No, thank you, sir. I am not ready to give up on the CIA. Your commencement words still ring in my heart and my soul."

"Good. Good. I'll be in touch." It was a lie. At that moment I had no intention of telling him a thing. Ever. I knew beyond most doubt that if I ever did tell him about Utoka or anything else I knew or even guessed, C. Harry Hayes would pump buckshot in me until I was dead.

We parted, probably forever, I assumed. I was almost to the door of the building when—unfortunately—my right hand felt a small card in my right suit coat pocket.

"Hold on one minute," I yelled back at Calvin Howell Youngfoot, who was moving swiftly south across the capitol lawn.

He came running. I handed him Tommy Walt's card. "This is my son's business. He needs a reliable worker."

He took the card and read it. "Grease collectors?" he said. Like it was the name of a wicked witch. Like the card was going to burn a hole in his hand. Like the card smelled of old restaurant grease itself.

"Only temporary," I said. "My son's a good young man just like you. He has his dreams too. He just needs some help getting started."

Calvin Howell Youngfoot looked again at the card for T.W. Grease Collectors. Then at me. And again at the card. He was a smart young man.

"If I gave this helping hand to your son, would you be more of a mind to keep trying to give a helping hand to me?" he said finally. He was a smart young man. I saw him as an example of Oklahoma education at its best. I could see Oklahoma Southeastern giving him the Distinguished Alumnus Award sometime.

"I follow the adage 'Forget who did you favors and you'll end up favorless and forgotten yourself.'" It was an adaptation of a Joeism.

"It's a deal," said the young man as he scurried away to call Tommy Walt at T.W. Grease Collectors.

I was pleased with myself for this stunning piece of inspired action. I had killed two birds with one stone. I had answered the knock of golden opportunity. I had turned a couple of sows' ears into silk.

Or as Joe, who was even more anti-Texas than he was anti-Arkansas, often said, I had turned Texas lice into Oklahoma linen.

And I figured that what C. did not know would not hurt him—or me.

·5·

The Utoka Sparrow

UTOKA WAS NOT my favorite town in Oklahoma. That was because of a sore experience I had had there right after I became lieutenant governor. It involved only one of its citizens, and of course it was unfair to blame the actions of one jerk on a whole town, but I couldn't help it. When I thought of Utoka, I thought of my sore experience with the Utoka Sparrow.

It involved a bus depot sign. I had heard from a Continental Trailways driver that a small red-and-white baked-enamel depot sign from the old Thunderbird Motor Coaches was still around there. I had grown up in Kansas with the Thunderbird and had even worked for it briefly as a ticket agent when I'd first come to Oklahoma. The Thunderbird had by now been bought out by Continental Trailways and there were few signs of its existence, of any kind, still around.

So for old times' sake, when my travels next took me to Utoka I set out to find the old sign. I figured it might look great over the fireplace in our den at home. Or even in my office at the capitol.

There was a young woman at the Utoka bus depot who said I should check with an old man named Hammer, now retired, who used to run the depot. Hammer sent me from his nursing home to three other people and locations before I ended up at the office of a young insurance man with no manners, sense or brains named Steve J. Sparrow. Yes, his building used to be the bus depot, he said. Yes, he found that old Thunderbird sign back up in the attic and, yes, he still had it. But, no, he would not let me have it for any price because he might want to paint over it and use it again to advertise his line of insurance. I explained what a sin against the motor coach history of America and Oklahoma it would be to paint over it, but he did not care. He was a jerk. One of those guys who was president of the high school student council and never quite got over it, even later as so-called adults. I could spot them a mile away, particularly in the legislature. They think the school bell's going to ring again any minute for them to address the student body on a new smoking-in-the-bathroom policy or some other Very Important Matter. The bell never rings again, of course. But the expecting keeps them jerks.

"Would you, at least, let me take a look at it and maybe take a snapshot of it?" I asked the Sparrow. "I've got a camera out in the car...."

"That wouldn't be possible," said the Sparrow. Like he was a deputy second assistant to the deputy third assistant

vice-president at the bank turning down a car loan application.

I had not told him I was the lieutenant governor. Now
I wanted to. Now I wanted to put my nose to his nose and
say, "I hereby inform you that I am the lieutenant governor
of Oklahoma, the Second Man of the Sooner State. You have
annoyed me, a crime for which you must be punished. I am
now going to return to Oklahoma City to issue orders that
everything about you and your insignificant insurance business be investigated up to the limits of all laws of the State
of Oklahoma. You will be ordered to surrender your Oklahoma driver's license. Your cars will be stripped of their
Oklahoma license plates. Your tax returns will be audited.
Your right to attend all OU and OSU football games will
be revoked. Your right to sing 'Oklahoma, Where the Wind
Comes Sweeping Down the Plains' will be terminated."

I was not that kind of person, of course, and I said nothing,
of course. I just took my soreness and quietly left Utoka and
that Thunderbird sign.

The soreness never went away. It was right there with
me and my curiosity as I drove into Utoka now to take a
look at the Sooner Spy. It was barely still daylight, exactly
eight days after I got the "Ask Jackie" clue. I was aching
to go before, but I had nothing on my schedule that took
me anywhere close. Then I got lucky. Harlton Gaines, the
mayor of Gainesville, dropped dead while presiding over a
city council meeting about resurfacing four streets in the
southern part of his town. He was in his early seventies
and had suffered from a heart condition, so it was not that
tragic or unexpected. Also, he had been slow in endorsing
Buffalo Joe in his first race for governor, so Joe asked me

to represent him and the People of Oklahoma at the funeral. Gainesville was thirty-five miles the other side of Utoka. I was delighted.

JackieMart–Utoka, it turned out, was just two buildings down from the Sparrow's insurance office. They were on the main north-south road through town, which was both U.S. Highways 69 and 75. The roads joined together at Denison, just over the Texas border, moved north as 69/75 through Utoka, where they parted again, 69 proceeding northeast to Muskogee, 75 straight north to Henryetta and Tulsa.

Like all JackieMarts, this one was a model of beauty, innovation and efficiency. I parked my blue Buick across the road from it and watched it go about its business. Like clockwork, customers drove to one of the drive-thru ordering microphones and then to the pick-up points for their blue plastic sacks of merchandise.

I drove through for a Grapette and a pack of narrow Fritos. The voice taking my order was female, sweet and friendly. My order was ready and waiting in the few seconds it took to drive to Pick-up Window #3. A delightful young man handed me my Grapette and Fritos in a blue plastic sack, took my money and gave me change. I strained to see inside. There was an older man in there. The Sooner Spy? I drove around and back across the street and parked. And consumed my order.

After a while I was back at an ordering station. A tube of Crest and a comb, please. The man was still in there. Definitely in charge. Good-looking guy. About my size, five-ten or so.

I came back around a third time a little later and bought

a blue spiral notebook and a ballpoint pen. The guy was in his forties. Good build.

My fourth time through was for a *Tulsa World;* the fifth, for a Milky Way candy bar. The man was clearly the boss.

And clearly the Sooner Spy? Certainly. But he didn't look *that* Russian. Whatever looking Russian really looked like. He may have even had his appearance changed to Oklahoma American. They could do things like that, I knew.

I was planning a sixth trip through the drive-thru when I saw the Utoka Sparrow. From where I was parked I could see the front door of his office as well as that of the JackieMart. It was just after six. There he was, walking out the front door with two young women. The sun was on its way down but I could still see clearly. I recognized one of the women as his secretary. The other was probably his full-time cheerleader. Two bits, four bits, six bits, a dollar, all for the Sparrow, stand up and holler!

I wanted to gun my car and run him over. Hi, Sparrow, remember me? The guy who wanted to preserve the antique bus depot sign for the good of humanity?

His departure did give me an idea. I figured that maybe I had already called attention to myself too much with the JackieMart people. Maybe it would be smart to move my car down to the four-car lot in front of the Sparrow's office.

So I did. I was sitting there in my Buick a few yards from the building. A few yards from a building that had at one time been a Thunderbird bus depot. A building that still had in it somewhere an old Thunderbird bus depot sign. One of those oval red-and-white baked-enamel signs that were pieces of art when they were made and were incredibly valuable historical objects now. An incredibly historical object that was doomed. Doomed because the man who had possession of it was a historic-insensitive jerk. A jerk who should not be allowed to deface and destroy artifacts of American transportation. Who was he to make that kind of decision? Aren't all Americans responsible for preserving our history? Didn't I have a responsibility to step forward and prevent defacement and dislocation of this nation's historical and artistic riches? A responsibility that superseded whatever infractions of law might possibly be involved? Sometimes there are drumbeats to be heard that call us to do things that involve huge risks. But who was it who said: "Take risks. Be willing to put your mind and your spirit, your time and your energy, your stomach and emotions on the line"?

I removed a small tool kit from the trunk of my car and went around to the back door of the Sparrow's insurance office. With a screwdriver, a coping-saw blade and some luck, the door opened quickly and quietly. There was still enough dusk light to help me move quickly and quietly. The office consisted of a bathroom and three other small rooms. An office for the Utoka Sparrow, a cramped one for an associate and a waiting room–reception area for a secretary.

A car stopped outside. I froze. No. It must have been across the street. What would I tell a policeman or anybody else who walked in? Hello, I am the lieutenant governor of Oklahoma. I am in the process of burglarizing this place for an old bus depot sign. If you could stop back by later I will be glad to give you a full statement. I'm a little busy right now, however.

In less than two minutes, I found the sign. It was stuck back in a hallway clothes closet underneath a pair of rubber boots, a snow shovel and a stack of several old Utoka phone books.

The sign was dusty and had a few rust pockmarks, but it was a thing of beauty. It was just like the one that had hung in front of the drugstore that was the bus depot back in my town in Kansas. THUNDERBIRD, it said in large red script across the top of the oval. There was a red-and-white thirty-seven-passenger Thunderbird Aerocoach in the center. BUS DEPOT was across the bottom half of the oval. The sign was about two feet long, eighteen or so inches high. It was heavy enameled steel and weighed probably ten or twelve pounds. But it felt light as cotton as I quickly and quietly took it out to my car. I wrapped it up in a blanket left over from a family picnic and stuck it under my suitcase in the Buick's trunk.

I had planned to spend the night in Utoka. But with that sign in the trunk I decided to go on to Gainesville for the night. Or should I forget Harvey Gaines's funeral and high-tail it back to Oklahoma City? No. Risk it. There was a nice Best Western in Gainesville on Highway 9 South. That would be fine.

It was a thirty-five-minute drive, but it seemed like thirty-five centuries.

I saw the headline in *The Daily Oklahoman:* "Lt. Gov. Nabbed in Utoka Bus Depot Sign Burglary—Claims Insanity." In the *Tulsa World:* "Lt. Gov. Is Bus Depot Sign Thief." I went through my "No comments" to the Associated Press, United Press International and the Oklahoma News Service. Then my explanation to the judge: "Your Honor, please believe me when I say I meant no harm. I was only trying to preserve for our children and our grandchildren a piece of their history."

I did enjoy thinking about the look on the face of the Utoka Sparrow when he eventually discovered that the sign was missing. I enjoyed the look on my face when I saw that wonderful sign on the wall of my den. I hated the look on my face when I explained to my four children why I had committed a felony. I teared up when I thought about having to resign my position as the Second Man of Oklahoma in order to escape impeachment. I stuttered when I pleaded with my father, a captain in the Kansas State Highway Patrol, to please forgive me for besmirching his good law enforcement name. It was an act of sudden criminal insanity, Dad. Like a bolt of lightning, an evil spirit moved inside my otherwise pure and law-abiding body and soul and told me to break and enter that office, to take the property of another for my own, to put myself above the laws of Oklahoma, to commit a sin against the precepts of human decency.

I could imagine what Buffalo Joe might have to say as he washed his hands of me now and forevermore. Probably something like, "Sorry, Mack, but a man in public life who doesn't know when to ditch a liability ends up in a ditch himself. Or being ditched himself. In a ditch or being ditched. Either way, Mack, it's over. Sorry, Mack. Consider yourself ditched."

My good friend C. would want to take his .38-caliber police revolver and blow a hole right between my eyes. Or more correctly, between my right eye and the empty socket where the left one used to be.

It was a stupid, terrible thing that I had done.

But it was not the first time I had committed the crime of burglary. The first time also involved buses. Years before, when I was a kid, I had broken into the bus depot in Lufkin, Texas, and taken a copy of *Russell's Official National Motor Coach Guide*. It's a long and different story, and I was never caught or found out.

Now it had happened again and I could only hope and pray for the same end result.

They gave a Class AAA funeral for Harvey Gaines. He and his family had always owned pretty much most of Gainesville, so the turnout was pretty much most of Gainesville. Schools, banks, city hall, and the courthouse were closed, and trash and garbage collection were suspended for the day. The 9:00 A.M. service was held at the Sarah Leona Gaines Memorial Baptist Church, which was the size of two gymnasiums; but there still wasn't room for everyone so the music and the words and the crying were piped outside on public address systems. It was an open-casket service. Harvey had been dressed in a dark gray suit with a light white stripe, a white shirt with French cuffs, and a dark red tie. His face was made up with rouge and lipstick so he looked like a plastic-doll version of Roy Rogers.

As I sat in the front row watching Harvey lying there, I decided I might just see about outlawing all open-casket funerals when I became acting governor of Oklahoma in a few days. On the grounds that they were disgusting.

The motorcade to the cemetery just outside of town was historic. I heard somebody say he had counted 175 cars and pickups, which would make it the longest funeral motorcade in Gainesville history. He said the record up to then was 130, when Harvey's mother, Sarah Leona Gaines, had died twelve years before, at the age of eighty-seven.

I was in the Buick and on the road that went back through Utoka to Oklahoma City by eleven. My mind was rid of Harvey Gaines and open caskets. It was back on what an awful person I had become, which was the subject of every waking thought I had had since I'd driven away from the Utoka Sparrow's insurance office with that hot bus depot sign in my trunk. In the first place it was stupid to have made such a big deal of coming to Utoka just to look at the Sooner Spy. Then it was insane to have let my soreness about a bus depot sign get hold of me. I was embarrassed to be myself. Just thinking about what I had done made my face warm.

I figured it would probably stay warm for the rest of my life.

Then at the city limits of Utoka I saw the familiar Rotary Club sign, the yellow wheel with its spokes of service and dedication. Under it were the words: "Meets Thursday, 12 noon, Best Western–Utoka Inn." It was Thursday, it was almost twelve noon and I was a loyal Rotarian. I had been in Rotary for well over ten years, since I'd first been elected county commissioner in Adabel. Each Rotarian has an occupation category and only one member from each category was allowed in each club. The Rotary was very tough on attendance. Miss so many meetings a year and you were put on probation. Don't clean up your act and you were out. It was something I paid attention to, because the headline "Lt. Gov. Gets Boot by Rotary for Bad Attendance" would not be helpful. Not as bad as "Lt. Gov. Nabbed in Burglary," but pretty bad. Being out of town was not an acceptable Rotarian excuse either. You were permitted—expected, really—to attend the Rotary Club meeting wherever you were. The out-of-town club would then notify your home club that you had attended. That's why, as you drove into most towns in Oklahoma and Kansas—maybe other states too, for all I know—there were those little round Rotary Club signs that said when and where the Rotary met. That was to help visiting Rotarians find their way.

Why not take a break from thinking about my awfulness and go to Rotary?

I found the Best Western–Utoka Inn, parked and went right on to the meeting room. There was a table in front of the door, with two men sitting there. I showed them my Rotary International membership card and bought a $5.50 luncheon ticket. They were delighted to see me, particularly after they realized I was the lieutenant governor.

"We don't usually get lieutenant governors just dropping in like this," said one of the two men, who introduced himself as Bill Hagood. His badge said his occupation category was Banking—Consumer. "We are honored and pleased to have you, sir. I'll be wanting to talk to you about our Globe Project while you're here."

Globe Project?

"What are you doing in Utoka?" asked the other man.

"Just passing through," is what I said. Spying on a Russian spy at the JackieMart and burglarizing a local insurance office, is what I did not say.

* * *

Bill Hagood escorted me to the buffet line. The food looked fresh and hot. First-class Rotary. Veal cutlet, mashed potatoes and brown gravy, green beans, Parker House rolls and pats of margarine, mixed salad with Thousand Island dressing, cherry cobbler and a choice of coffee, iced tea or milk. I took iced tea. The cobbler and the salad were in separate small bowls. I took some of everything else, and it made for a full plate and a full load to juggle.

Against the far wall was a head table with about ten places, and fifteen or so round tables with eight chairs were spread around the rest of the room. Bill Hagood pointed me toward one about halfway back from the head table. Six Rotarians were already there. They stood and introduced themselves and said how delighted and honored they were to eat lunch with the lieutenant governor of Oklahoma. I assured them the honor and the delight were really mine.

"Let's talk globes," Bill Hagood said just before the first bite of veal cutlet was in my mouth.

"Globes?" I replied.

"Look up there on that wall," he said, pointing toward a big streamer sign behind the head table that I had not noticed before. Painted in Rotary colors, blue on golden yellow, were the words "Put Utoka on the Globe."

"Look there," he said, pointing to the center of our table. There was a small tin globe. "Look at all of the other tables."

I put my fork down and looked around at the other tables. There was a globe in the center of each.

"There are something like 546,000 globes of the world sold in this country every year," said Bill Hagood, a crew-cut blond man of forty-five or so in a nice dark blue suit, white shirt and green tie. "There are huge ones like what the president uses in the Oval Office at the White House. There are cheap ones that are plastic and blow up like balloons. Expensive ones that light up and change colors as you twirl them around. Some are made out of tin, others glass, others curved papier-mâché. You can buy them for as much as four thousand dollars or as little as seven-fifty. You can get them so small you can hold them in the palm of one hand. You can get them so huge it would take a semi, a crane and the U.S. Army to unload. But you know something, Mack? Do you mind if I call you Mack? I understand everyone does. . . ."

"Mack is all I like to be called. . . ."

"Mack, there is one thing all of these thousands of globes have in common, no matter their size or their price. Do you know what that is?"

Roundness?

"None of them have Utoka, Oklahoma, on them," he said. "Not a one of them."

He paused as if he had just delivered a monumental piece of news. Like: Tomorrow at dawn Oklahoma becomes a part of Arkansas. Or: The game of baseball no longer exists. Or: Jesus himself is giving the invocation and has just taken a seat at the head table.

"Is it because Utoka is too small?" I asked, finally, breaking the emotional moment.

"Exactly," he said, "and that is the catch. In order to get larger we must get on the globes. As long as we are not on the globes we stay small." He pointed to the streamer sign. "Put Utoka on the globe and we put Utoka on the map. Get it?"

I got it.

He grabbed the small tin globe from the center of our table. "Look at this, Mack. Look." He pointed to the United States. His right forefinger went to Chicago. "Chicago," he said. "Then, look, there's Kansas City." Right. "Now down here is Dallas. And up here is Tulsa. Over there is Oklahoma City." Right. "Now, right about there on this is where we should be. It should say 'Utoka.' Right there." His finger tapped down hard on the little tin globe. "It is our mission in this Rotary Club to get Utoka on the globe where it belongs. It is the Globe Project. Will you help us?"

"How?"

He had not taken a bite of his lunch yet. I had managed only a few myself.

"We are in the process of contacting all the globe manufacturers. There are twenty-three major ones and twenty-one small ones. We are going one on one with each of them. Each Rotarian in this club has an assigned globe manufacturer. We are writing letters and making phone calls and dropping in unannounced..."

I held up a hand of caution.

"Bill, remember, I am the lieutenant governor of all of Oklahoma. How could I single out Utoka for a place on the globes of the world?" I took the small tin globe from him. "Look at this. Muskogee isn't on here either. Neither is Enid or Ponca City or Adabel or Durant or Hugotown..."

"Durant doesn't deserve a place on a road map, much less on a globe."

"I could not play favorites among the cities and towns of the Sooner State."

I was following one of Buffalo Joe's major rules of politics: "Always say no first, Mack. Somebody asks you for a light,

75

say no, even if you've got a pack of matches and a dozen lighters in your pockets. Same if somebody asks you to support their bill, their highway, their son, their candidate, their budget, their God. If you later change your mind, even if it's a minute later, and say, 'Yes, fine,' they think they talked you into it. Always say no. You say yes and you can never change your mind. Never. Go back on a yes, you're a lousy, no-good politician. Go back on a no and you're a hero. Got it, Mack?"

I got it.

"Sure," said Bill Hagood. He turned his attention to his veal cutlet and mashed potatoes. He was disappointed and unhappy with his new friend, Mack, the lieutenant governor of Oklahoma.

The whole thing reminded me of a man I called the Map Man. I ran into him by accident many years ago when I was wandering around after I first left Kansas. The Map Man collected road maps. He tore off corners of them so he would always have a piece of Kansas, Texas or wherever. He lived in Joplin, Missouri, and I actually went to his house and saw his collection of maps. They were stacked all over his basement. They were of all states and locations and came from all oil companies and mapmakers. Some were very old and brittle, others fairly new. The man's real name was Marshall M. Mooney. I grew very fond of him even though he never looked anybody in the eye except on rare, special occasions. The saddest thing about him was that his wife, Gertrude, was dying of cancer and she sent him around Oklahoma, Kansas, Missouri and Texas to find people to whom she had done bad things during her life and apologize to them. I helped him settle a couple of accounts. I used to think about him a lot and wonder whether he was still alive and how he was doing. But he had not crossed my mind in years.

Bill Hagood, the Globe Man of Utoka, was very different from Marshall M. Mooney, the Map Man of Joplin. But also very similar. What was there about maps and globes that touched people so strongly? And strangely?

It was time for the meeting to start.

The pastor of the Trinity Lutheran Church of Utoka, not Jesus Himself, gave the invocation. He was a tight-voiced man of around forty who wore his dark brown hair ever so slightly down over his ears. He asked that all of us, our food, our work and our families be blessed by the Lord Jesus Christ. He asked that Jesus be in the dugout, on the field and behind the plate for the Utoka Southeast Oklahoma Gas and Light Mustangs in tomorrow night's crucial semipro game against Durant's Wapanucka Feed and Supply Company Warriors. We all joined him in saying a vigorous amen. We turned to the American flag just to the right end of the head table—to our left—to recite the pledge of allegiance to the flag of the United States of America.

It was then that I saw who was at the head table. The Russian. The Spy. The Sooner Spy. There he was. Standing there with the rest of them at the head table in front of the huge Rotary flag with our motto, "Service Above Self." Standing there with his right hand over his left breast repeating the pledge of allegiance to the flag of the United States of America!

We finished with those wonderful words: "One nation,

under God, with liberty and justice for all."

The Sooner Spy turned back to the front. I couldn't keep my eyes off him. Our eyes met. He nodded but did not smile. I smiled but did not nod.

I sat back down. Oh, what a stupid thing I had done coming to this Rotary luncheon! I had done it without thinking. It was a reflex. Out of town on Thursday, the day my club met in Oklahoma City, so go to the local Rotary Club wherever I was. Automatic. I had been doing it for years. I saw the little round sign and I did it again this day without thinking.

Without thinking. Without thinking that I had stolen property in the trunk of my car parked outside in the Best Western–Utoka Inn parking lot. "Lt. Gov. Arrested at Rotary Club Luncheon for Burglary—Goes Quietly but Pleads for Time to Finish Veal Cutlet and Mashed Potatoes."

Without thinking that the Sooner Spy might be a Rotarian.

"The man at the head table in the blue suit and pink tie," I whispered to Bill Hagood, "he looks familiar but I can't place him. . . ."

"That's Art Pennington. He's our Rotary president. Runs the JackieMart here in town."

"I hope there are no plans to introduce me publicly or anything like that," I said quickly.

"Sure thing, Mack. We always introduce our visiting Rotarians. Those are the rules, you know that. I'll do the honors for you," he said. "It's not often the lieutenant governor of Oklahoma drops in for lunch like this. It's an honor even if you won't give us a hand with the globes."

"Yes, I understand. But there is a problem. I am going to have to leave. Now, in fact. Right now. Just two more bites or so and then I must be on my way. The business of governing our Sooner State never stops. Sometimes not even long enough for a good Rotary lunch."

He smiled. He understood.

I wolfed down another bite of just about everything and disappeared down the side of the room and out the door as fast as I could.

I had gone three, maybe four steps outside the meeting room when I heard a voice behind me.

"Mr. Lieutenant Governor! Is that you?"

There was no way to do anything but stop. I turned around. A man carrying a napkin and chewing on a mouth full of veal cutlet came toward me. It was the Sooner Spy.

He was in his early fifties. Tall, solidly built. Dark skin, black hair, heavy black mustache. Non-Oklahoma voice. Like young Calvin Howell Youngfoot's. Impressive.

He stuck out his hand. "I thought I recognized you from your picture. I'm Art Pennington. I'm president of the club and a business associate of your wife's."

"Yes, well, it is a pleasure," I said.

His eyes were as dark as his hair. And they were pinned right on my own. "I own the JackieMart here in Utoka," he said, as if he were a movie star announcing the winner of an Academy Award. His button said "Art." His category was Grocery—Drive Thru.

"What brings you our way?" he said.

"A funeral over in Gainesville."

"I see...."

"Well, nice to meet you," I said. "I am on my way back

79

to Oklahoma City now and, as usual, running late. Sorry I can't stay for all the meeting."

I waved and moved out and on into my Buick.

I saw in my rearview mirror that he had followed me outside. He stood and watched as I drove out of the parking lot.

·6·

Find the Drive-Thru Rotary

I STOPPED in Shawnee at a Derby Oil station pay phone and called my office. I told Janice Alice Montgomery where I was and that she should expect me in the office at about three o'clock.

"Better not come right here," she said. "Better you go directly to Director Hayes's office over at the OBI. He called here a while ago to say it was so urgent he see you in person that he could barely find the words to express it. You know how Director Hayes is."

Yes, I knew how Mr. Hayes was.

I assumed that somehow C. had found out I had burglarized the Utoka Sparrow's office. He was going to confront me with the evidence and a warrant, handcuff me, fingerprint me, jail me, disgrace me, ruin me.

It was all over. My life as I knew it and loved it was over.

Janice Alice ran through the other calls. Most were from people who had ideas for my eleven days as acting governor of Oklahoma. "Several want you to fill the vacancy on the Oklahoma Supreme Court while the governor's gone. They even gave me names of their nominees over the phone," she said. "Can you imagine?"

I could imagine. Maybe the thing to do with these kinds of appointments was to sell them openly and publicly to the highest bidder. What is a supreme court seat worth these days? Do I hear $10,000? Going once, going twice. How about $15,000? Or maybe have a big ceremony on statewide television to open the bid envelopes, as for the Emmys and Oscars, with accountants standing by to keep everything honest. The winner, the new associate justice of the Oklahoma Supreme Court, is the Honorable Arthur Sylvester Jones of Pawhuska! Three cheers for Arthur Sylvester Jones of Pawhuska!

I had more serious matters on my mind. I was about to have my very own life and future openly and publicly snuffed out.

I drove right to the OBI office at 36th and Eastern. But instead of being arrested for burglary and theft of a bus depot sign I listened with C. to that tape of the telephone call from the CIA man who was threatening to twirl C. around by his one good ear.

I had asked C. to relax. But he hadn't relaxed. The kids' word for it is "spastic." C. was spastic.

"The clue! I should not have given you that clue! I should have known you would have figured it out! Fool! Fool! Fool! I am a fool! The only bigger one in Oklahoma than you! Me! Idiot Number One! Fool!"

"I don't understand the problem, for God's sake...."

C. screamed: "The problem is, that man in Utoka is a resettled defector! He was the KGB station chief in Washington! There's a death sentence out on him!"

"Oh, my," I replied.

I did not want to go to the office. Not right away. I needed to think. I needed some quiet. I needed peace. I pulled the Buick out of the OBI lot onto Northeast 36th Street. But instead of turning west toward the capitol I gunned it to the other side of the street to the 45th Infantry Division Museum. I pulled the car into the parking lot next to the tanks, howitzers, helicopters, field ambulances and armored trucks and got out.

The 45th was the Thunderbird Division, Oklahoma's division. General George Patton said about it: "The 45th is one of the best, if not actually the best, division in the history of American arms." Its ranks were originally drawn exclusively from Oklahoma, but through the years and wars soldiers from many other states ended up wearing the red-and-yellow Indian Thunderbird patch of the 45th on their left shoulders. The building had been converted from a National Guard armory into the best kind of museum: small, uncrowded, full of real things such as flamethrowers, gas masks, pistols, rifles, machine guns, mess kits, canteens, messenger bicycles, medals, shoulder patches, uniforms and other equipment used by soldiers in various wars, including one they called the War of Rebellion, otherwise known as the American Civil War.

There was a display case full of what one Oklahoma City soldier had hauled away from Adolf Hitler's apartment in

Munich. Table coasters, crystal, silverware, stationery, linen napkins, pillowcases—all with the initials "A.H." on them. Right in the center of the display was a large black-and-white photograph of the soldier lying on Hitler's bed in his full combat uniform reading a copy of *Mein Kampf.* The picture had originally appeared in *Life* magazine on May 14, 1945.

The men of the 45th had also liberated a concentration camp in the summer of 1945. The one at a place called Dachau. There under glass were photographs of the awfulness they found. I had never been able to really look at them.

There was a special area commemorating Thunderbirds who had won the Congressional Medal of Honor. Miniature toy soldiers represented each Thunderbird soldier doing whatever he did to win the medal—attacking a sniper's nest, German bunker, tank or whatever. Each display was about eighteen inches square and looked like a tiny movie set you could play with. It was good the Marines didn't have such a museum in Oklahoma City. I would not have liked for them to have such an awful reenactment as Pepper's being blown to bits by a hand grenade in Korea.

Maybe it was because of Pepper that I came to the museum so often. Since I had only one eye, I had not been allowed to join the armed forces. Pepper had been my best friend and was married to Jackie when he jumped on that hand grenade. Jackie had been pregnant with Tommy Walt and Walterene when he died. I had always loved Jackie, so it was natural and perfect and wonderful that we then got married and I became Tommy Walt's and Walterene's father.

I felt a tap on my shoulder. "Sir, I hate to bother you."

It was Calvin Howell Youngfoot. He was dressed in coveralls like the ones Tommy Walt had on in his warehouse. His face was drawn, his hair was not very well combed. He smelled like fried chicken.

"Your secretary said you were coming to the OBI and I saw you come over here, so I thought I would presume to join you," he said in that unusually well-spoken manner of his. Grease work had changed his appearance but not his talk. "I hate to keep bothering you, but I was wondering if there was anything you could tell me. Anything at all. It does mean so much to me. Particularly now."

"Particularly now?"

"Look at me, sir. I am a mess. I am a greasy mess. I have grease in my hair and under my fingernails and in my ears and in my nose and between my toes and in my pores. I bathe every night with every strong soap available. But it will not come out. It will *never* come out. I am sure of that. I will go through the rest of my life smelling like a piece of Kentucky Fried Chicken or an order of fries. You asked me to help out your son. I am doing that. Every night I am out there with him in that truck, pouring grease into drums and cleaning drums and washing up the truck and the floor of the warehouse. Have you talked to Tommy Walt? Ask him. He will tell you that I am the finest worker it would be possible ever to find. The absolute finest. I am making a tremendous sacrifice of my time and personal hygiene now and in the future in order to do this for him."

"Good," I said.

We walked into the main room of the museum. My eye was caught by the face of a mannequin dressed in the uniform of a World War II lieutenant in the German army. His face was soft and pink and did not fit that of a Nazi killer.

"You remember what you said about not forgetting who does you favors," he said. "I think the time has come to remember, sir. I really do. I have lived up to my end of the bargain. Now it is your turn, sir. If you will please excuse my bluntness."

I looked at him again. The well-groomed Calvin Howell Youngfoot really was a mess. He really was undergoing an awful experience being an employee of T.W. Grease Collectors. And he really did have me. We had a deal. But there was no way I could honor it. Not now. Not with a man's life at risk. This wasn't any little game of my curiosity and his job-seeking anymore. This was serious. But so was my word. I had to tell him *something*. All right, then I would. Something honest but completely harmless that would get me off the hook. And that would be the end of it.

"I will give you a clue, Calvin," I said. It was the first time I had called him by his first name. It seemed appropriate. Natural. "One clue."

"Thank you, thank you."

"One clue. One clue only."

What one clue?

We had stopped to look more carefully at the Nazi uniform.

"Find the drive-thru Rotary and you'll find your spy," I said.

I do not know why I said it. It just came to me standing there. It had no connection to the Nazi mannequin or anything else. Find the drive-thru Rotary and you'll find your spy. It was also an unbreakable, indecipherable clue. No way Calvin would figure it out. No way anybody could. It was perfect.

Calvin made me say it again.

"Is that all there is, sir?" He was excited. Really excited.

"That is all there is."

He grabbed my right hand and shook it. "I will find him, sir. Thanks to you, I will find him. 'Find the drive-thru Rotary and you'll find your spy.' Yes, sir."

And away he went.

Outside in the parking lot a few minutes later, I stopped for a look at a jeep that was used in World War II. They were wonderful little vehicles, those jeeps. I remembered them well from war movies. Robert Taylor always had one.

Calvin Howell Youngfoot came rushing up to me. I saw that he had left his car running and the door open a few feet away. It was a nice-looking car, a dark red Chevrolet Impala four-door. Not bad for a recent college graduate employee of T.W. Grease Collectors.

"Are you sure there is nothing else?" he said to me. He was breathing hard.

"I'm sure," I said.

"I can't figure it out."

"Think about it some more. It'll come."

"I don't know where to begin."

"The CIA isn't interested in people who throw up their hands after a couple of minutes and say, 'I don't know where to begin.' "

"You are right, sir. You are right."

He gave me a little wave of a salute and raced back to his waiting dark red Impala.

I felt bad about what I had done, but I had no real choice. It would have been wrong to give him a solvable clue. Very wrong. It would also have been wrong not to have given him something. Very wrong. I had worked it out the best way I could.

I had never met or even seen a picture of a real CIA agent before in my life. But it would be hard to imagine a more perfect one than David Donald (Colley) Collins. About six-one, trim, muscular, athletic. Caramel skin, slicked-back dark brown hair sprinkled with gray. Arkansas accent sprinkled with smarts and class. As impressive a man in his mid-fifties as I had ever met.

C. had gone to the airport by himself. I waited for them in one of the private dining rooms at the Park Plaza Hotel, which C. said was the tasteful Mr. Collins's favorite place to do business. The Park Plaza's restaurant called itself by the French for "snail," *escargot*. L'Escargot. Its main attraction was its five small private rooms, each named after a bird. Ours was the Meadowlark Room. The walls were covered with wallpaper with yellow and brown meadowlarks on it. Each room was large enough for a table of eight, but tonight, for us, there was a smaller table with three chairs and three places set. The white linen tablecloth was heavy and thick. So were the silver and the glasses.

There was no finer place to eat in Oklahoma. Not even in Tulsa. It was very expensive. C. said Collins would be picking up the tab. He always did, because CIA agents have unlimited expense accounts.

Collins could not have been nicer and friendlier to me. He started by asking me about myself and how I came to be the Second Man of Oklahoma. I gave him a short version of my life. Born in Kansas, came to Oklahoma in my early twenties, got elected county commissioner in Adabel, Oklahoma, by luck, and then became lieutenant governor, also pretty much by luck. He asked about family. I told him about Pepper and Jackie and the kids.

I asked him for his life story and he gave me an even shorter one. Born in Camden, Arkansas, three years in the Army as an intelligence officer, and since then in what he called "civilian government service." He made it sound as if he worked for the Commodity Stabilization Service.

I ordered a well-done slice of prime rib, green beans in an almond sauce, and a tossed green salad with blue-cheese dressing. C. had a sliced veal dish of some kind, and Collins went with some awful thing with a French name that was cow kidneys. He had snails to start with. C. chose onion soup, which seemed awfully hot for the season. I had some melon with the thinnest-sliced ham I had ever seen.

We were well into our main courses and a second bottle of red wine when the subject of the Russian spy in Utoka came up.

Collins did it up with a polite, quiet question to me: "Do you travel to Utoka often, Mr. Lieutenant Governor?"

"No, not really. Only when I have a reason."

"C. tells me your reason last week was to observe a Russian spy, is that correct?"

"Yes and no."

I told him the story of Calvin Howell Youngfoot. The commencement speech. His dream of being a CIA agent to serve his country. His turndown. His determination not to take no for an answer. His dedication to the task of making

89

the CIA see that he was a brilliant spy prospect. My desire to help him not only because of my desire to help all young lost Oklahomans find their way but also because of what I had said in my commencement address. I repeated some of what I had said. Particularly the moving parts about taking risks, of never counting yourself out and down. I felt an obligation to do what I could. So this idea of his finding a real Russian spy in Oklahoma came up. C. gave me one small clue and I got lucky and found the spy. I said I had a natural curiosity that would not let me rest until I had actually laid eyes on the guy.

"Not many Russian spies come along here in Oklahoma," I said, "and as lieutenant governor I thought I owed it to myself and to the people to see the one we had."

"Why did you park across the street and spy on the guy all afternoon?" Collins asked. Still very quietly and politely.

"I wanted a good look, I guess. But I know I really do not have a good explanation. It was stupid. No question about that..."

"Why did you run away from him at the Rotary meeting?"

"No reason, really. It just didn't make sense to say anything. It made sense to get out of there and out of Utoka."

C. started talking. Thank God. It was obvious he had already gone through most of it at least once with Collins. Here it came again.

"*I* plead stupidity of the first order, Colley. I should never have said a thing to Mack. But Mack here is absolutely reliable. The most reliable and trustworthy public official I have ever dealt with in all of my years in law enforcement. He and I have worked on several sensitive projects that involve the utmost of discretion, nerve and secrecy. I should not have even given him a clue, though. I admit that. But I emphasize and reemphasize as strongly as I know how that no harm can possibly come from my stupidity. Please be assured that the security of your man in Utoka has not been breached. His cover has not been blown."

Collins said: "I hear you, C. I hear you and I want to believe you. But these resettled, new-identity cases are high risk. The highest of the high risk. This guy in particular. The other side would love to find him and dispose of him more than probably any other we have. A lot of effort went into altering his appearance and placing him where he is."

"You mean the Russians might kill him?" I asked.

"I mean kill him, yes sir. Or maybe get him to re-defect in a big public to-do. Either way is fine with them. If they find him he either goes home loudly or dies quietly."

"Did you settle him in Oklahoma because he would be hard to find down here?" I asked.

"No, it was his idea. This is where he wanted to live," said Collins.

"Why?"

"Oh, I don't know. He just did," he said, making it clear he did not want to say any more.

"There's got to be a real reason. A Russian spy wouldn't decide to live in Oklahoma for no reason." I had to know.

Collins sighed as if to say, All right, but this is it. "I think his mother back in Mother Russia was a Broadway musicals freak. She had several records of them that she played all of the time for her son on their little Victrola. One of them was *Oklahoma!*"

"Can he sing the songs?"

"Right, sure. Right."

"That's amazing. Think of it. A Russian spy going around singing the songs from *Oklahoma!*"

"What a lovely Oklahoma story," C. said without much conviction.

"Yes," said Collins. "A very lovely Oklahoma story."

"Why Utoka?" I asked, pressing my luck.

"We had a contact there," Collins said.

"Please, Mack," C. said. "No more questions."

"Why JackieMart?"

"He wanted to run his own business. I called my old friend C. He suggested a JackieMart. We went through regular channels from then on. Now that is it. Not one more drop of information."

"Not a drop," I said.

Two waiters came into the Meadowlark Room and removed our main-course plates. They replaced them with our salads. The French eat their salads after the main course for some reason.

The waiters left us in private again.

We went on to other subjects for a while. C. got me talking again about all the crazy things I might do the next week when I became acting governor. Collins was fascinated by the fact that I would actually have the full powers of the governor for those eleven days. I could call out the National Guard, appoint, veto and do all the things governors normally do. But with the legislature not in session and very little else going on, it did not appear to be adding up to much this time. The main problem was just fending off fruitcakes and their fruitcake ideas.

The waiters rolled an elaborate dessert cart into the room.

I chose what they called an éclair, which was just a pastry in the shape of a fat finger with a yellow cream pudding inside and chocolate icing outside. C. had a piece of lemon pie. Collins passed on dessert and went straight to coffee, which was served to all of us in tiny little cups with handles that were hard to grasp.

I tried to get Collins to tell us about his life in the CIA, but it did not come easily. Where all had he served? I asked. Mostly in Europe and the Far East, he replied. How did he happen to end up in Dallas? There are six liaison offices around the country. They are staffed by "old hands" who are no longer considered ripe for field work. What kind of field work did you do? All kinds. Is it dangerous work? Not really. Is it exciting? Mostly.

"I really do wish you would put in a good word for this young Calvin Howell Youngfoot," I said. "He seems ideally suited to me for your kind of work."

He took out a notebook and wrote Calvin's name in it.

"The CIA doesn't discriminate against American Indians, does it?" I asked.

"I can't imagine such a thing," he said. "If there is such a policy, I am not aware of it. I know for a fact that I have never been ordered to go out and find an American Indian to discriminate against."

I liked Collins. I could see why he and C. were friends. A waiter came in with a box of cigars but we all declined to take one. None of us smoked. Soon another waiter came in with a check on a small silver tray. Collins took care of it by signing his name and room number at the bottom.

It had been a mostly pleasant evening, despite the problems with the Russian spy, despite the fact that C. and I had jeopardized the security of the CIA's resettled Russian defector. Despite the fact that he had come to Oklahoma City prepared to wring C.'s remaining good ear, if necessary.

We were at the door to the private room. I was back asking regular, personal Oklahoma-type questions.

"When will you retire?" I asked Collins.

"Soon, maybe."

"What will you do then?"

"Emigrate to Oklahoma and run a JackieMart drive-thru grocery," he said. He was kidding, of course.

"Jackie has just decided to expand into Arkansas," I said, playing along. "The first one's going to be in Arkadelphia. I'll put in a good word for you if you'd like."

We were out in the hotel lobby now.

"Well, I hope you have forgiven C. for his little indiscretion," I said as I shook hands with Collins "There is no way young Youngfoot will ever find the man in Utoka. The clue I gave him this afternoon was a mind-breaker. No way..."

"Clue? What clue?" Collins leaped to my side.

"Mack. No!" said C. "You didn't give him a clue? No!"

With one of them on either side of me, I walked into the men's room off the lobby. It was late; no one was there. Collins turned on two faucets at the sink. C. dashed around and flushed all the toilets and urinals.

"What clue did you give him?" Collins asked in a lowered voice of controlled anger.

" 'Find the drive-thru Rotary and you find the Russian spy.' "

"What does that mean, Mack? What in Christ's name does that mean?" C. was spastic again.

"The Russian in Utoka is president of the Rotary. His Rotary classification is Grocery—Drive-Thru. It came to me as a clue this afternoon at the 45th Infantry Division Museum. Youngfoot found me there. He's doing me a favor by helping Tommy Walt with his grease collection business so I felt like I owed him. He wanted a clue so I just made that up off the top of my head and gave it to him."

There was silence—except for the flowing of water from the faucets. C. flushed the toilets and the urinals again.

"How smart really is this Youngfoot?" Collins asked.

"He seems real smart. But I don't think he's smart enough to figure that out. I really don't."

"We can't take a chance," he said. "Find him first thing in the morning and tell him something else. Give him another clue. One that takes him far off the trail. Way, *way* off of it."

"Will do. I certainly will do that. Yes, sir."

We walked together to the parking lot behind the hotel. We passed the rear entrance to the kitchen and a little open shed of tin drums that resembled those in Tommy Walt's warehouse.

It had been one of the worst days of my life. But at least now it was over. Or so I thought as I pulled the Buick into our garage, turned on the garage light and closed the door. Then I opened the car trunk and removed the Thunderbird sign. I felt like a wanted felon. Like a cat burglar hiding the loot. A Sooner Jack the Ripper, disposing of a victim. I found another old blanket and wrapped another layer around the sign. Then, using a stepladder, I stuck it in the farthest corner of a storage bin up above the washing machine and dryer. It had been years since anybody had even looked up there for anything.

It was almost ten forty-five. I knew Jackie would already be asleep. She liked to be at JackieMart headquarters every morning at seven-fifteen, so that meant early to bed. She had left the light on in the kitchen and there in the center of the kitchen table was a note, under a bottle of catsup.

Mack—

Tommy Walt needs you. It's an emergency. Said to call no matter how late. Call at his office.

How was the funeral?

I love you as much as always,

Jackie

Funeral? I had almost forgotten about the going of Harvey Gaines of Gainesville. What a day it had been.

I had no choice but to call Tommy Walt. I used the beige phone right there on the wall by the kitchen door.

"T.W. Grease Collectors," came the voice of my son after only one ring.

"Hi, son . . ."

"Dad. Dad! What did you do to Calvin? Where did he go?" He was screaming.

"I didn't do anything. . . ."

"He called and said he wouldn't be at work tonight or ever again and you knew why."

"Well, it's too long a story to tell at this time of night. I am sorry if he quit. But he was there only temporarily anyhow. You knew that. He wants to be a CIA spy. You knew that. He came to help you out as a favor. You knew that. I am sorry if it presents you with a problem. . . ."

"Problem? Dad! I have to make my pick-ups! I am already almost an hour late! I can't do it alone! I must have a helper! It takes two people! Dad! I am ruined!"

So the worst day of my life was not over yet.

We were in Tommy Walt's green International Harvester pickup on the way to our first stop. It was at a seafood place called Santa Fe, which made no sense. A restaurant named Santa Fe should serve Mexican food not fish. Seafood places should have names like Captain's Table or Ahoy Inn. I wondered what the Santa Fe Railroad thought about a fish restaurant calling itself Santa Fe. I wanted to say all of that to Tommy Walt but he would not have been interested. He was worried into a feverish silence. I assumed he was worried that we couldn't make all the pick-ups on time and that he would lose his contracts. Worried about what using his father as a helper did to his need for him to make it in business on his own.

I was wearing a pair of official T.W. Grease Collectors coveralls. Plus a pair of heavy work gloves. Plus the oldest blue workshirt I owned. Plus my oldest and scroungiest pair of washable sneakers.

We turned up the alley to go up behind Santa Fe. The headlights picked up another truck way up ahead. Tommy Walt flashed his lights a couple of times, honked his horn, turned to me and said, "Hold on," and floorboarded it.

By the time we got to the rear of Santa Fe, the other truck had sped out and away through the other end of the alley.

Tommy Walt screech-braked us to a stop. He jumped out.

"They got one of them!" he yelled. "But the other two are still here. The bastards! Thank God."

The bastards. Thank God?

Each of the two remaining drums was filled to the top with fifty-five gallons of liquid grease that had been used to fry fish. Each drum weighed over four hundred pounds. We slipped rods from a hand truck under the drums and then rolled them to the rear of the International, where we pushed them onto the hydraulic tailgate that lifted them to the back of the truck. Lots of grease that had been used to fry hundreds of pieces of catfish, trout, bass and other assorted fish spilled and slopped and splattered on my shirt, my coveralls and, of course, my gloves. We replaced the two full drums with three clean empties we had brought from the warehouse.

And we jumped back into the truck like race-car drivers finishing a pit stop at Indianapolis. Tommy Walt gunned it out of the alley and we swung up the street at top speed toward our next stop, Billy Wayne Jordon's Shakes and Fries.

"All right, son," I said once we were under way. "What's going on here? Are we stealing this grease or what?"

"No, sir. That's our grease. Those other guys were stealing our grease. It's ours to pick up by contract. They're grease pirates."

"Grease pirates?"

"They're hired toughs. They run in packs. Come in and steal other people's grease. The rendering plants look the other way and buy it anyhow. This is a rough business, Dad.

A lot rougher than I ever imagined. They're trying to scare me out. Calvin and I have been fighting them every night. Last night they dropped big concrete blocks into several of our drums. The night before they punched holes in a few drums. If I can just hang in there and show them I'm in to stay . . . well, I'll be fine and well on to making my thirty-five thousand a year."

Billy Wayne Jordon's Shakes and Fries had only one drum out for pick-up. It had not been tinkered with. A large, runny, smelly plop of grease fell onto my left pants leg as we loaded it. It had an aroma of fries, burgers and hot dogs that almost drowned out the smell of fish.

Thank God?

Stop three was a Kentucky Fried Chicken. The pirates had beat us there. And had just left. Instead of stealing T.W. Grease Collectors grease, they'd just tipped over its two drums. Grease was running like a small stream down the alley to a gutter in the street.

"Sorry, Dad" said my son, "but we're going to have to clean this up. That's our grease."

I looked down at Our Grease and thought of all the various parts of chickens it had recently transformed into the pride of Colonel Sanders. I wondered if Colonel Sanders was still awake down there in Kentucky. I wondered if he would take a call this late at night from the lieutenant governor of Oklahoma. Hi, Colonel, just thought I'd report a crime at your south Oklahoma City franchise. Some grease pirates came by a while ago and tipped over two fifty-five-gallon drums of grease. It's created a real river of grease out to the street. Ever seen a river of grease, Colonel?

Tommy Walt hooked up a hose to an outside faucet. I

grabbed a broom and helped the stream move more quickly to the street. The grease and water went above the soles of my sneakers. I felt the moisture inside my shoes, down between the toes. Ever felt Kentucky Fried Chicken grease between your toes, Colonel?

We made three more pick-ups without incident. Il Sorrento, an Italian place that apparently did a lot of veal work, supplied one full drum. Two more came from two Chinese places, Chiang Charlie's and Hunan Heaven Northside.

Then we headed for R. & R. Rendering. I wondered for a second who was the first and who was the second R. But only for a second. It was after two in the morning. I now smelled and felt like a fifty-five-gallon drum of grease. Grease that had been used to fry a veritable symphony of cuisine from the popular Sooner-American diet. "Veritable symphony" was how Buffalo Joe sometimes described things he didn't like. This bill is a veritable symphony of greed. That newspaper columnist is a veritable symphony of pomposity. That state representative is a veritable symphony of ignorance.

A couple of half-awake men from R. & R. using motorized dollies and hand trucks removed the full drums of Our Grease from the back of the truck, weighed them, took them off somewhere to empty them and then came back with a check for Tommy Walt.

There had been an unfortunate incident on the way to R. & R. Rendering. The shortest route from Hunan Heaven Northside was right through downtown. There was no traffic, so that was the way we went. About a block away from the Park Plaza it occurred to me that the route was going to take us right behind the hotel and the kitchen entrance. Where there were two drums of grease.

I said something to Tommy Walt about it.

"That's not our grease, Dad. Sooner State Grease Collection, Incorporated, has the Park Plaza contract."

"It's just sitting there," I said. "We could just stop and quickly put it in back. Nobody would ever know the difference. It would help even the score for what you lost to the pirates tonight. . . ."

"Dad! That would make us pirates too! We'd be criminals! You are the lieutenant governor of Oklahoma!"

Oh, yes, that is who I am.

·7·
Probably Choctaw

I WAS IN the office at the regular time the next morning. Eight o'clock. I had had barely five hours' sleep. The rest of the time since I'd left Tommy Walt had been spent in a hot shower, where I'd tried in vain to rid myself of the smell and feel of grease. I now knew what Calvin had been talking about. I knew it was in me to stay. There would always be a faint whiff of fried chicken and french fries about me. Always and forevermore. I told Tommy Walt I could not help him again. Ever again and forevermore. He said he would call a temporary-labor place first thing the next morning.

The first thing I asked Janice Alice Montgomery to do was to get Calvin Howell Youngfoot on the phone.

She was back at my office door a couple of minutes later. "That number doesn't work," she said.

"What do you mean, 'doesn't work'?"

"I mean I dialed it four times and a recording comes on which says, 'The number you have dialed is not a working number.'"

"Here, let me see it."

She handed me a white index card. In her handwriting was Youngfoot's name, plus her note, "O.S.S.C. graduate—wants help on job," with the number. I dialed the number.

"The number you have dialed is not a working number. Please check your directory for the correct number or dial for assistance from an operator," said a recorded female voice.

I dialed again and she said it again.

"What about his address? Did he leave us his address?"

"No, sir," said Janice Alice.

Now what?

"Call my son and ask him for Calvin's phone number. You must have written it down wrong."

"Yes, sir." She said it in a way that let me know there was no way she had written that number wrong.

In a minute or two she was back with the proud news that the number Tommy Walt had for Calvin was the same one we had. "He was asleep and was not happy to be woken up," she said.

"Too bad," I said. "Call Oklahoma Southeastern in Hugotown. They'll have his home address and phone number."

"Yes, sir." Janice Alice had been with me since I became lieutenant governor. She had worked for years as an aide around the corner in the governor's office and was just what I needed. She was happy to do, without complaint, the typing and other administrative work that fell to me. I liked her even though she had a maddening habit of inventing stupid nicknames for people. She used to call everybody Dove. I finally cured her of that and after a while she came up with "Pet." Everybody was Pet. She thought it was cute. I put up with it a few weeks and said enough to stop her. Now she had individual names for each person. Buffalo Joe was Joey. The speaker of the house, Luther Wallace, was called Killer, because he was good-looking and because he had been a Marine officer back in the fifties. The only good thing was that she had not made up one for me.

In a few minutes she was back at my door. Her face was flushed, as with a fever.

"I have the Oklahoma Southeastern dean of students on the line," she said. "His name is Ransom. You had better talk to him yourself. He's on two-eight-three-five."

I picked up the phone on my desk and punched down the button for extension 2835.

"This is the lieutenant governor," I said.

"Yes, sir. Dean Allen Ransom here, sir. We are still talking about that stirring commencement address you gave. I for one have never heard a better one and, believe me, in twenty-seven years in the education business I have heard a lot of commencement addresses. You spoke forthrightly about taking risks, you spoke about issues and matters that are relevant to our students and to all youth at this particular time in their lives and at this particular time in this state's and this country's history...."

"Thank you, Dean. Thank you very much. Tell me about Calvin Howell Youngfoot."

"There is nothing to tell, sir. We have no record of anybody by that name having attended this school."

"Come on now," I said. "He just graduated. He went through the receiving line. That's where I met him. He was in a gray suit and blue tie. I am sure he was in the graduating class. Probably near the top of the class. He's smart as a whip."

"Sir, I am looking right now on my desk in front of me at a list of those who graduated. There are no Youngfoots. No Calvins. Not even any Howells. Besides, I take great pride in the fact that I personally know every member of every graduating class. There was no Calvin Howell Youngfoot in that class."

"Could he have graduated under another name?"

"People normally graduate under their own names, sir. What did he look like?"

"Dark skin. Indian. Black hair, black eyes. Good build. Handsome. Probably Choctaw."

"Sorry, sir. That rings no bells. I really am sorry. Why is it so important, if I may ask?"

"Sorry, Dean. It's Top State of Oklahoma Secret business."

"I didn't know there was such a thing."

I heard and felt some commotion at my office door. I looked up and there they were—C. of the OBI and Collins of the CIA. Janice Alice, acting very much afraid, slipped around them and out. C. closed the door behind her.

C. and Collins were not happy. C.'s one-eared head and face normally had a good, clean, dark gray cast to match the gray suits he always wore. Right now his face seemed a bit more whitish-gray than usual.

Neither sat down. I stood up.

"We wanted you to know immediately and in person that I just a few minutes ago got off the phone with our personnel people in Washington," Collins said. "They have no record of anyone named Calvin Howell Youngfoot ever having applied for a job with us."

"Could he have done it under another name?" I asked.

"People do not come to work for us under names other than their own. That comes later."

"Did you call him off Utoka, Mack?" asked C.

"No, not yet."

"Why not?"

"I haven't been able to locate him this morning," I said.

C.'s face was now a bleached white.

I kept talking: "The phone number he left does not work. It's not a real one. My son doesn't have any other number either."

"What does Tommy Walt have to do with this?" C. asked. His voice also was now almost pure white.

"Remember? Calvin was working for him as a helper in his new business."

"What business?" Collins asked very quietly.

It was difficult to say the words but I was not about to lie. I said: "The restaurant grease collection business. I mentioned it at dinner. I was up half the night filling in for Calvin, in fact. It is the toughest, dirtiest work I have ever done. If you take a deep sniff you'll probably pick up a whiff of fried chicken and fries and maybe some catfish...."

Collins gave me one of those hell-must-be-next looks. C.'s eyes carried the message: Shut up, Mack! Please!

But I kept talking. I had to.

"We also checked at Oklahoma Southeastern. I met him

there, remember, when I was making the commencement address. He was in the graduating class. That's what I assumed, at least. Well, it turns out they don't have a record of him down at Oklahoma Southeastern. I just hung up from talking to the dean of students.

"Something's wrong, I'm sorry to say. I know something's terribly wrong. I do not know what's going on here, but something is certainly not adding up. . . ."

Collins turned again to C. He raised his right hand in front of him, put his thumb and forefinger together and started twirling his hand around in a circle.

Like he was twirling a one-eared person around in the air by his one remaining ear.

In less than an hour we were in the OBI's Cessna Skywagon on the way to Utoka. I was along because C. and Collins decided they might need me. If they were able to find the young man calling himself Calvin Howell Youngfoot I might come in handy. They said the word "handy" with the same kind of emotion and warmth they would have used to describe a pair of pliers. Or a screwdriver. They said there might still be a chance for me to sidetrack him, to turn him toward some false lead and thus keep the Sooner Spy protected and safe.

The plane was a two-engine seven-seater. Smitty, C.'s young agent assistant, had stocked it with hot coffee and chocolate-covered cake doughnuts, the only things C. ate before lunch. Collins sat with C. up in the front right behind the pilot and they talked between themselves. I sat in the rear by myself. C. was one of the best friends I had in the world, but he had gone with Collins on this. Like kids

choosing up sides for a pick-up softball game. He had chosen
Collins's side. I didn't blame him but I did not like it. Collins
was upset, so C. was upset. Every time Collins frowned, C.
frowned. I, his dumb lieutenant governor–politician friend,
had embarrassed him in front of this superman from the
CIA. Maybe I would have felt the same way if C. had done
a similar thing in front of someone I respected. Maybe.

At first, I just said, Sorry, oh, sorry, C. Please forgive me,
Mr. Collins. I am so stupid. I am so dumb. I am such a
moron. But after a while I stopped all of that. What I had
done was no more stupid than what C. had done in telling
me about the spy in the first place and then giving me the
"Ask Jackie" clue. And what he had done was no more
stupid than what Collins had done in telling C. about the
spy in the *first* first place. My dad, a captain in the Kansas
State Highway Patrol, always told me to remember there is
no such thing as a secret. Once two people know anything,
it's all over. Sometime, somewhere, under some circumstance
one of the two will tell another, who will, in turn, sometime,
somewhere, under some circumstance tell another. And so
on and so on. "Secret," he said, was a label, not a thing. It
meant fewer people knew it than nonsecret things but that
was about all.

Right, Dad.

The only conversation C. and Collins had with me on the
plane was right before landing. They came back where I
was and for about the hundredth time asked about the clue
I gave Youngfoot.

" 'Find the drive-thru Rotary and you find the Russian
spy,' " C. repeated once more. "Are you sure that was all
there was?"

108

"Absolutely one hundred percent sure."

"Are there Rotary clubs in the Soviet Union?" C. asked Collins.

"I have no idea."

"No," I answered. "I am a Rotarian and I know for a fact that there are none."

"So maybe he'll never figure it out? Maybe he's out there driving through all the traffic circles or freeway interchanges in Oklahoma looking for the Russian spy?" Collins said. "They call traffic circles 'rotaries' in Europe."

"It's possible," C. said. "He'd have to be a first-class triple-A genius to figure out the real answer. Tell us again how smart he is, Mack."

"I don't think anybody is smart enough to figure out that clue," I said. "I really don't."

Collins said nothing.

We were met at the Utoka Municipal Airport by two OBI agents in an unmarked black four-door Mercury sedan. The airport consisted of a one-story administration building and two large tin-roofed hangars just west of town on Highway 75. The only planes that landed there were small, private ones like the one we were on. Utoka had no regular airline service.

The agents told C. all was peace and quiet in and around the JackieMart. The Sooner Spy had gone to his store in the morning and had remained there. There had been no incidents, and no young men meeting the description of Calvin Howell Youngfoot had appeared, either at the store or in and around Utoka.

A few minutes later another small plane landed on the runway. Collins went over and met it after it had taxied up to the administration building next to our plane. It was a five-seat Beechcraft. Four men wearing dark suits, white shirts and narrow ties and carrying briefcases jumped out. Collins talked to them by the side of the plane for five minutes and then brought them over to C. and me.

Three of them he introduced as FBI agents, the fourth he gave only a name to, no affiliation. I guessed that he was CIA. All four were between thirty-five and forty-five, tanned and healthy. Collins asked if I would accompany one of the FBI men and the CIA-probable to an office inside the airport. They had some pictures they wanted me to look at.

Each had a set of photo albums, containing mostly black-and-white five-by-sevens of young men. Some were traditional police mug shots or portraits, others were clearly blowups from group photos and snapshots or were taken in restaurants, on the street or elsewhere. None of them was labeled. Neither of the agents told me who the men in the photos were or why I was looking at them. All the FBI man said was: "Please look at these as closely as you can, sir, and tell us if you see the man you have come to know as Calvin Howell Youngfoot." "Take as much time as you wish," said the CIA-probable.

There were maybe a hundred or so photos in all to look at. I went through them all twice, some of them a third and a fourth time. Calvin Howell Youngfoot was not there.

"Look again, please, for nose or eye characteristics that may have been similar," said the FBI agent. "It is possible there might have been some appearance modification."

I did as he asked, going through most of them once again. Still nothing.

"Is there any picture that while definitely not of Youngfoot bears any resemblance to him, no matter how remote?" the CIA-probable asked.

There was one. It was of a young man of swarthy or dark complexion with black eyes. He had been photographed, obviously without his knowledge, while looking intently at something directly in front of him. There was no way to tell what he was looking at. The camera must have been surreptitiously planted in the middle of whatever it was. A painting at a museum? A sign at a bus stop? A flower bush in a park? A book in a library or bookstore? A mannequin in a clothing store window?

I went back through one of the albums and found the picture.

"He was dark-skinned like this man," I said. "I assumed he was an Indian, particularly with the name Youngfoot and all."

"That's what you were supposed to think, obviously," said the FBI man.

"This particular guy is an Afghan," said the CIA-probable.

"What's an Afghan?" I asked.

"Somebody from Afghanistan. It's a Soviet satellite state. The KGB occasionally recruits from there. That's probably where your man came from."

It was finally said out loud. Calvin Howell Youngfoot was a Russian agent. Surely on a mission to find, kill or neutralize the defector who liked the music from *Oklahoma!*

·8·

Father of the Year

I T STARTED raining. A light, sweet, straight-down Oklahoma rain. A soaker. The kind wheat farmers in the Panhandle get down on their knees in Baptist and Holy Road churches to pay their respects to. I had glanced at the forecast in *The Daily Oklahoman* on the plane coming down. "Partly cloudy skies, slight chance of precipitation," was what it said.

Partly cloudy skies, slight chance of precipitation. How many times had I been told that just before the sky fell and I was suddenly sitting at my desk in wet socks? The weather people on TV were the worst. A state representative from Hollis once introduced a bill that would hold TV stations financially liable for agricultural damage that resulted from an erroneous TV weather forecast. It was a delightfully silly thing and Luther Wallace and I easily got it killed in committee, but not before Luther, a Southern Baptist, had some fun scaring the wits out of a few TV station owners. The speaker of the house particularly enjoyed telling the owner of the Tulsa CBS outlet that if we were unable to hold back the tide on this one, there was no telling what might come next. "It would be a terrible day for Oklahoma, an absolutely terrible day for Oklahoma if this God-fearing crazy legislature of ours got it in their heads next to try to hold you responsible for the drunkedness and maiming and death that occur from all of those beer commercials y'all run night and day."

The rain calmed things down a bit. So did the fact that Calvin Howell Youngfoot of the KGB had not blown into town yet and tried to spray the Sooner Spy and/or JackieMart–Utoka with machine-gun fire. Collins and C. became more normal. Especially C. He even kidded me about my becoming acting governor: maybe this would be the time for me to make my big move, to do something dramatic such as call the legislature into special session and force it to vote on something far out like a handgun control law. Gun control was C.'s main hobbyhorse. It made no sense to him as someone responsible for stopping crime in Oklahoma that a simple law restricting and regulating the sale of pistols could not be passed unanimously and with glorious enthusiasm by any body of people who professed to be operating in the public interest. "Only the uninformed, the idiots, the criminals and the politicians oppose gun control," he said. "And only the smart, the sane and the ordinary citizens support it, so it'll never happen. Particularly as long as the gun industry keeps feeding millions to those creeps at the NRA." He said it over and over. And over and over.

Luther and I agreed with him, but Buffalo Joe and an overwhelming majority of our legislators and voters did not.

Collins remained mostly smiling, quiet Collins. His annoyance with me and C. and the situation was always there, but mostly in his dark brown eyes. I did not know that much about CIA agents, and most of what I did know was probably stupid and overly dramatic and wrong, but I must tell you his eyes seemed ready to rendezvous with secret agents, commit murder, plant bombs, bug offices, swim icy rivers, steal state secrets, scale tall buildings and do all kinds of other spy things. Risk It things. I still liked him. I was glad he was on our side.

I knew things were really better because C. and Collins did not go off and have lunch without me. I was invited to join them, C. style, in the backseat of the black OBI Mercury. C. said he would treat us to Big Macs and fries and milk shakes. It did not surprise me when Collins passed on the fries and the shake. He had a cup of black coffee with his Big Mac.

We cruised Utoka while we ate. It seemed to me that the town had suddenly doubled in population. There were little clusters of men in khaki work clothes on many corners, plus lots of telephone and electric linemen climbing on poles and peering down manhole covers. The JackieMart had a steady stream of white male customers. I didn't ask, but there was no doubt they were mostly OBI, FBI and CIA men.

The hardest part of the cruising was going by the Utoka Sparrow's insurance office. The scene of the crime. Had he opened the closet yet? Had he noticed the sign was missing? Had he reported it to the Utoka police? Had they come and investigated? Did they find any clues? Had someone reported seeing a car parked outside? Had they written down the license number? Had it been traced to a somewhat prominent state official?

It got so relaxed with C. and Collins as we drove and lunched that I decided to give them the benefit of my wisdom before I returned to Oklahoma City. It seemed clear Calvin was not going to show up anytime soon, and I had to prepare to assume my duties in the morning as acting governor of Oklahoma.

"Why not just put your man and his family in a fast car out of here?" I said. "Why take even a remote chance that Calvin, or whatever his name is, might find him?"

"It's not that simple, Mack," C. said.

"Yes it is." I turned to face Collins, who was sitting between C. and me. "If you have a target you don't want hit, then move the target. Why don't you go now and get the guy and get him out of here? Move him somewhere else in America. He must have a second favorite Broadway show. What about Iowa? Does he like *The Music Man?*"

Collins looked at his coffee and then at me and said softly: "That is not my decision."

"Whose is it?"

"Washington's."

"There's no decision to make, really. It's the only thing to do. It makes no sense to just sit here like this. . . ."

C. leaned over to the OBI agent behind the wheel. "Run us back to the airport." Then to me, "I'll have our plane give you a ride back to Oklahoma City. You must have a lot of work to do before tomorrow. Sorry about the rain. Maybe the pilot can fly around it."

"Right. Thanks," I said.

"If you need us," C. said, "we'll be either at the Best Western or at the Utoka PD."

"What should I do if Calvin contacts me?" I said.

Collins, his voice still calm and restrained, said, "Please give us a call. Say nothing to him. Nothing, please."

"He's long gone from Oklahoma by now, isn't he, Colley?" C. asked.

"Maybe not. There's no reason for him to think we're on to him. Who knows?"

At the airport, I asked C. to join me for a private minute in the administration office before I got back on the Cessna. He excused himself from Colley and we both dashed through the rain to the building.

"Do you know anything about a group of grease pirates operating in Oklahoma City?" I asked him once we were inside.

"Grease pirates? Come on, Mack...."

"They're hired thugs who go around stealing legitimate collectors' drums of restaurant grease, among other terrible things. The deal is to intimidate and harass honest businessmen and drive them out of business."

"Honest businessmen like Tommy Walt?"

"Exactly."

"I told you it was a rough business. I'll get Smitty or somebody back at the office to check around."

"Thanks, C."

Then he did a loud sniff of his nose. "Do you smell catfish grease around here?" he said. "Maybe it's Big Mac grease. Or Whopper grease. It's grease, though."

I laughed. "It's in my hair. It'll be there for the rest of my life." We shook hands.

He said: "Sorry if I haven't been that friendly, Mack. This is a real mess here with the spy. Colley has his job to do and so do I. You and I have managed to really screw things up. I must do everything I can to unscrew them. Good luck tomorrow and for the next eleven days."

He clapped me on the shoulder. A good man, this C. Harry Hayes.

He turned to head back outside to the car and to Collins.

"You haven't got something else to tell me, have you, Mack?" he said.

Heat shot up from my toes, through my crotch, stomach, chest and neck right to my face.

"No, C. Why?"

"Nothing. I thought there might have been something else."

No. There was nothing else.

I watched the soft rain hit the tiny Cessna window all the way back to Oklahoma City, the whole hour we were in the air. It made me think of those agonizing Saturdays in Kansas when it rained and we could not play baseball. All Saturdays from April to September were *for* baseball. I used to sit at the kitchen table and watch the drops hit the window and try to watch it stop. How about right now? How about after twelve more drops? Will it be too wet around the plate to play? What if it stopped this very split second? Could we still play? What about right now? Maybe if we threw some sand around the bags? How about this split second? My mother always told me that rain was like chocolate fudge. Watched fudge never hardens. Watched rain never stops.

My mother died suddenly, of a burst appendix, when I was twelve. It was something that I never got over. Do you know people who ever got over their mother's dying when they were twelve? The day I was sworn in as lieutenant governor of Oklahoma, I really missed her. What's the point in becoming lieutenant governor of Oklahoma if your mother's not around to know it? I thought of her again on the flight from Utoka because of the rain and because she wasn't going to be there again when I became acting governor of Oklahoma the next morning.

An OBI agent in an OBI car drove me from the downtown airport to the capitol. The combination of the grease pirates by night and the Russian spies by day had done me in. I wanted to go home and go to bed. But I had to make an appearance at the office; and my blue Buick Skylark was parked at the capitol.

Janice Alice had four important messages for me. The first was from Tommy Walt. "He said it was important that he talk to you as soon as possible."

No. No, I resolved. No. No, no, no.

No!

"Hi, Dad, thanks for calling. Where have you been? Mom said something about an emergency trip to Utoka. What kind of emergency could there ever be in Utoka? Well, look, I haven't been able to find somebody who's up to . . ."

"No, son. No. I cannot do it tonight. I really cannot."

"Dad, you were great last night. You're a natural. You really are. Think of it as an adventure. Us against the grease pirates. If you can do it just one more time . . ."

"No, son. No."

There was a tick of silence. Then he said: "Why not, Dad?"

"I am going to take over as acting governor of Oklahoma tomorrow for eleven days."

"Yeah, but this is tonight."

"Tommy Walt, please. I have to get ready. I have to get rested. I cannot stay up the whole night . . . well, you know."

"Yeah, I know. Stay up the whole night fooling around with old restaurant grease. It's messy work and you wish your son wasn't in it. I know. You are embarrassed that I am a grease collector. I know. No son of the acting governor of Oklahoma should be in the restaurant grease collection business, should he? Yeah, I know."

And he hung up.

I did not call him back.

No! The second message was from somebody named Horace T. Anderson, who was president of the Will Rogers Chapter of the Jaycees in Claremore and this year's state Jaycee president. "He said congratulations. You have been chosen as the Oklahoma Father of the Year. The Jaycees were particularly moved by the way you have raised children of a dead Marine hero as your own. A special plaque and certificate will be given to you on the Friday before Father's Day at the State Jaycees Convention in Tulsa. If you cannot be present, a special delegation of Jaycees will come to your office and make the presentation in front of the capitol press corps at the capitol building in Oklahoma City. Again, congratulations."

No!

The third was from Bill Hagood in Utoka. "He said he had just heard that you were going to be the acting governor for the next eleven days, starting tomorrow. He wondered if you would consider signing a proclamation for Put Oklahoma Towns on the Globe Week. He said he understood why you did not want to single out Utoka only, but what about the whole state? What about getting behind an effort to get many more towns in Oklahoma on all globes everywhere? He said that way Utoka would be bound to be helped but not in a way that appeared that you were showing partiality."

No!

The fourth call was from Calvin Howell Youngfoot. "He just asked to talk to you. I told him you were gone for the day. I was careful to ask if you could call him somewhere. I knew from this morning from that business with Mr. Hayes and the other man that you very much wanted to know where he was, but he said no. He said he would be back in touch with you."

I would not have been too surprised if there had been a fifth call: "A man who identified himself only as the Utoka Sparrow said he knew you were the one who stole his old Thunderbird bus depot sign. He said he was going to get you." I asked Janice Alice to get C. on the phone. She found him at the Utoka Police Department. I told him about the call from Calvin.

He was back to me in two minutes to say: "Colley's checking Washington. If he should contact you before then, just don't say a thing. Stall. Say nothing."

"Shouldn't I go ahead and give him another clue that will throw him way off the Utoka trail?"

"No, Mack. Don't do anything like that. No. Wait for instructions. No."

No?

The executive committee of the Oklahoma Grocers' Association was having a dinner meeting at the Sheraton Park downtown. Jackie was the board representative for all small convenience-type stores so she felt an obligation to go. That meant she was not there when I got home or when I went to bed and fell sound asleep.

It was impossible for her to come into our bedroom or any other room without making noise and commotion. I became aware through a half-awake haze that she was in the bathroom and then at her dressing table in the bedroom.

After a while I heard and felt her get into bed. She turned out the light. And snuggled up to my back.

"How was the dinner?" I whispered.

"I didn't know you were awake." She kissed the back of my neck. "Boring. A Piggly Wiggly lobbyist from Washington talked about commodity price controls."

"Mmmmm."

"What color is Tommy Walt's grease truck?"

"Green."

"International?"

"Yes."

"I think I saw him rolling a barrel from out behind a Burger King a while ago."

"Was he alone?"

"I didn't see anybody else. But somebody could have been in the truck or somewhere else. Did he get somebody to replace the lieutenant governor of Oklahoma?"

"I don't know."

"You have got to help him, Mack."

"I've already done enough."

"One of our salesmen said he heard on the radio that you have been chosen Oklahoma Father of the Year by the Jaycees. Is that right?"

"Yes."

"Congratulations. I just hope the word doesn't get out that you wouldn't help your son through a tough time in the restaurant grease collection business."

She leaned across and around and kissed me on the lips. "Good night, Father of the Year."

I had not opened my eyes or mind during all of this, so by a count of about twenty I was back in that presleep haze.

But Jackie had one more item on her mind.

"Are you still awake? A young man showed up at our office late this afternoon. He said he knew you. His name was Big Foot, Little Toe, something Indian. He wanted to know if we had any drive-thru stores on traffic circles. He called them rotaries...."

I was awake.

"Then he wanted to know if any of the managers knew all of the words to the songs in *Oklahoma!*"

I sat up and turned on the light on the table by my side of the bed.

"Did you know of one?"

"Mack, what in the world?" She was stunned.

"Did you tell him the name of a manager who knows the words to the songs?"

"No. We checked everyone in the office. Nobody could think of anybody. Mack, what's going on? You're not still mixed up in that spy business, are you?"

I turned the light out and scooted back down under the covers. And did not answer.

·9·

Whipped Cream
and Dry Ice

BUFFALO JOE always made a big deal out of my taking over as acting governor of Oklahoma. The first time, he made me sit behind his desk in the governor's office while he personally took my picture with his own personal camera. His wife had given him a small Japanese camera, which he began to carry with him at all times. After a while it became a pattern at all Buffalo Joe events that at some time he would pull his camera out of his pocket and take pictures of everybody and everything involved. Prints of the pictures he took were seldom seen afterward, however, and Luther had a theory that there was never any film in his camera, that nobody, not even Buffalo Joe, could afford the film and print costs of the hundreds and hundreds of shots he snapped. There were busy weeks when, it was safe to say, he snapped the shutter on his Japanese camera in public six to seven hundred times. Luther's theory was that Joe had simply figured out that there was nothing more flattering to a person than to have another person want to take his picture. And that was particularly true if the person with the camera was the governor of Oklahoma and the subject was a member of the Oklahoma legislature or even just a voter from Muskogee or Perry or Cushing on a tour of the capitol building with his son's 4-H Club. What made me think Luther was right was that one time I had asked Joe for a copy of a picture he had taken of me and Harry the Cat Brecheen, the retired great St. Louis Cardinals pitcher, who was from Adabel. The Cat had come to Joe's office at the capitol to help kick off Oklahoma Little League Week. Joe never came up with the picture. The Cat was an old hero of mine and I really wanted the photo of the two of us together. I asked Joe for it several times. Eight different times, to be exact. The last time he said, "You know, the truth is, you shouldn't need a picture of you and The Cat, Mack. You were there. You were there in my office. You have the picture in your mind. It's there in your mind forever. It would cheapen the memory if you had a photograph. No, Mack, it's just as well those negatives disappeared. For your sake, it's just as well. A picture in your mind is worth more than a picture on a piece of paper."

To mark this acting governorship, he gave me a warm-up jacket with "Acting Governor of Oklahoma" emblazoned on the back, inside an outlined map of our state. "Mack" was embroidered in script over the left breast pocket.

"Wear it proudly, Mack," he said. "Wear it proudly."

I thanked him for the jacket and replaced my dark brown suit coat with it. He took my picture, from the front and the back. His secretary, Sylvia, and my secretary, Janice Alice, were the only other people present. They were also involved in a temporary transfer of power. While Sylvia would remain in the office to coordinate and oversee, Janice Alice would function as my secretary. They both now clapped for Joe and me.

Joe then took his briefcase, which was black leather with gold snaps, shook my hand and headed for the door.

"I know it goes without saying, Mack, that it is my confidence and Oklahoma's confidence in you that makes it possible for me to leave the state in a peaceful state of mind," he said.

"I thank you and Oklahoma for that confidence," I said.

He waved, and he was gone.

Buffalo Joe timed his departure and the little warm-up–jacket ceremony so my first duty as acting governor would be to take his place at the monthly Governor's Prayer Breakfast. I never discussed religion with Joe, but it always appeared to me that he looked upon it the same way he did elections: something terrible that must be endured in order to hold public office. He did all of the normal political things such as go to a Methodist Church every Sunday morning, invoke His name in most speeches but never in vain in public. But he was not what you would call a believer type. The only private thing he ever said to me about religion was, "God and politics go together like whipped cream and dry ice, Mack. Whipped cream and dry ice." Whipped cream and dry ice? It made no sense to me. Still doesn't.

The prayer breakfast was held in the Robin Red Wing Room on the second floor of the Park Plaza. I was running a few minutes late so I leaped off the hotel elevator. And turned right into the young man I had come to know as Calvin Howell Youngfoot.

"Good morning, sir," he said just like always. "I hope you don't mind my imposing on your time one more time."

"Not at all," I said. I did my best to talk and look the way I always did too. It was not easy. Here before me stood a dirty, rotten Russian spy on a death mission. I had never before in my life stood before such a person or dreamed that I ever would.

"I cannot break the clue," he said. "I can find no Russian spy. I was sure one clue would be enough. But I was wrong. Please, sir. Just one more. And I promise that will be it, I promise I will leave you alone forever."

Why did I not notice before how strangely this young man acted? His preciseness, his smoothness, his smarminess. Very un-Oklahoman, very un-Choctaw.

"They're waiting for me at the breakfast," I said cleverly. "I'll need some time to think of something. Where can I call you?"

"I no longer have access to a regular phone. I will contact you at your office, if that is all right."

"I will be in and out the rest of the day," I said.

"When do you think you might have something?" he said.

I looked down at my watch. "By noon. That's three and a half hours from now. I'll be at a crime commission meeting over at the Sheraton then. Meet me there."

"Great, sir. Thank you. And congratulations on becoming the acting governor."

"It's just for eleven days," I said modestly.

I watched him disappear into the elevator. There was a bank of pay phones down the hall. I called C. in Utoka and told him what had happened, and that if I had no instructions from him and Collins by noon, I would make my own decision on what to do.

And that would probably be in my capacity as acting governor ordering the Oklahoma Highway Patrol to arrest Calvin Howell Youngfoot as a Russian spy.

I left C. screaming "No! No! *No!*" into the phone and went on inside the Robin Red Wing Room for a breakfast of Danish pastries, scrambled eggs, bacon, orange juice and coffee, followed by some scripture and a Presbyterian sermon, with Luther Wallace and 125 other of my fellow Christian legislative, political, professional and business leaders of Oklahoma.

It was customary for the governor to give the closing benediction prayer. I thanked Him for everything, including the inspiration and strength for us all to play fairly and honestly and courageously in the politics and government of our Sooner State.

Amen.

One of the best things about being acting governor was the chauffeur-driven car. For eleven days I would be driven wherever I wanted to go and whenever I wanted to go there, in a dark blue Chrysler Imperial. The chauffeurs were Springer and Autry, two armed officers of the Oklahoma Highway Patrol in plain clothes. They called me Governor. Springer drove, Autry rode shotgun in the front passenger seat.

I was in the backseat on my way from the Park Plaza to

a water resources meeting back at the capitol when a message came through on Autry's two-way radio. It was urgent that I call a certain number as soon as possible. It was urgent that I do so on a pay phone. It was urgent that I understand the message was from Mr. Collins.

I had the car stop at a Texaco on Broadway, where I knew there was an outside pay phone. Away from prying ears. From eavesdroppers. From Russian spies. From assassins.

"Give the person in question forthright guidance," said Collins. He had answered the phone. The number was a Utoka area code but I did not know where in Utoka he was.

" 'Forthright guidance'?" I said. I did not get it.

"So forthright that he will be successful."

"At finding the target?"

"Correct."

"That makes no sense."

"It makes sense to the home office, Governor. You're not afraid of this guy, are you?"

"No."

"We'll have some help there if you need it."

"You mean agents posing as trash collectors and things? Great. None of this makes any sense. Why not just grab him now and stop the whole thing?"

"Do you fish, Governor?"

"Once in a while . . ."

"Congratulations on becoming acting governor."

"It's only for eleven days."

The Governor's Crime and Penal Commission meeting was what the newspapers would call a No Go Joe meeting:

the meeting wasn't over until Joe said it was. It was a device Joe had developed for getting state boards and commissions to reach decisions. He would call them into session and then announce they were going to sit around the clock until the issue at hand was resolved. The *Tulsa Tribune,* normally no fan of Joe's, called it a breakthrough in governing. *The Daily Oklahoman* said Joe had added an intelligent, innovative wrinkle to the concept of civil disobedience.

Joe always made a point of stopping by No Go Joe meetings. That duty fell to me when he was gone and that's why I went to the Sheraton.

The issue before the Commission was sex. There had been a mild uprising among the inmates at the state penitentiary at McAlester a few months before. One of their demands was for the married men to be able to spend the night with their wives every once in a while, as they do in some foreign prisons. Four small rooms were outfitted with a cot, and the prisoners' request was granted as an experiment for three consecutive Saturday nights. The results were mixed. There were fights when some of the women were turned away because the guards did not believe they were really married to the inmates they were coming to see. On the second Saturday a guard took a twenty dollar bill in exchange for letting a particular unmarried woman in to see an unmarried inmate. The woman was later identified as having a record of arrests for prostitution in Oklahoma City and Muskogee.

The question before the Crime and Penal Commission was whether to continue the program permanently. The meeting on the issue had begun the previous morning at eleven. It was now the following afternoon. Tempers were frayed. Attention was lacking. So was patience.

"Governor, this is ridiculous," the Commission chairman, a Pauls Valley banker in a black suit with a vest, said the moment I sat down at a place near the head of the table. "We cannot resolve it. We have heard from witnesses who claim the program is workable, we have heard from witnesses who say the program is a farce. We are split down the middle on whether to go ahead. You and Governor Hayman can make us stay here until the end of Oklahoma and we will never reach an agreement."

"I thought there were nine members of this commission," I said, ever so cleverly. When in doubt, goes a cardinal rule of courthouse politics, change the subject.

"There are supposed to be nine. But a seat has been vacant since the death of R. Marcus Tunlaw last month," said the chairman. "Governor Hayman has not appointed a replacement."

I had an idea.

I excused myself and went to a phone in the lobby. The deputy attorney general, a young man from Elk City with great potential if his boss was convicted by the feds as expected, came on the line immediately. I laid out the problem. He said there was a law that made the governor an *ex officio* member of all commissions. That meant he could vote. I said thank you.

I went back inside the meeting room, which was named after that great pitcher from Oklahoma, Carl Hubbell, and reported on my conversation with the deputy attorney general.

They were delighted. The chairman again put the motion to a vote.

"All in favor of making the Marital Visitation Program

permanent signify by saying aye. All opposed, nay," he said. "The secretary will call the roll."

The first two votes were aye. Then came a nay. Another aye. Two nays. An aye and a nay. It was 4 to 4. Then it was my turn.

The secretary, an attractive Muskogee woman accountant of sixty-plus, said:

"The governor."

"Abstain," I said.

"Abstain?" cried the chairman. "No," cried somebody else. "What's the point?" asked another.

"The point is," I replied, "I now move that the marital visitation question be delayed until the real governor returns or until a ninth real member is appointed to the board, whichever comes first."

There was a quick second, a unanimous favorable vote and an adjournment of the meeting of the Governor's Crime and Penal Commission.

Another cardinal rule of courthouse politics is: When in doubt, delay.

On the way out, there he was in the lobby waiting for me. The young KGB man, alias Calvin Howell Youngfoot.

I waved at him to follow me. We got into the backseat of the Chrysler Imperial. I told Springer to head for Utoka.

"That's nearly a three-hour drive, sir," Autry said.

"That's right," I said. "Stop at a pay phone at a JackieMart so I can make a few calls."

Then I turned to young Calvin.

"I have just given you your clues," I said. "I hope you were paying attention."

"I was. Thank you."

"Good luck," I said. "Where can we drop you?"

"Right here will be fine," he said. He was excited.

"Right here?" We were on Sheridan headed east from downtown to Lincoln Boulevard. There was nothing there but furniture and hardware warehouses.

The driver stopped the car. Young Calvin thanked me, shook my hand and got out of the car.

"I want to know where he goes," I said to the men in the front seat.

We went east two blocks and then turned right and circled back around, just in time to see young Calvin climbing into the front seat of a cream-colored Chevy four-door. A well-dressed older man was driving.

I could not help but notice also that there were delivery trucks and broken-down cars around, with men in them trying hard to look busy.

By the time we arrived at the capitol, Autry had information on his two-way radio that the Chevy was rented from Hertz by a man named J. Smith of Columbus, Ohio.

I called Collins and said only, "Forthright guidance given, per your instructions."

"Thank you, Governor."

"What happens next?"

"Thank you, Governor." And he hung up.

·10·

Service Above Self

I TRIED my best to put the Sooner Spy and Calvin Howell Youngfoot out of my mind and go about my business as acting governor of Oklahoma.

A group of dental technicians came into the office for the signing of a proclamation declaring Margaret Beth Riley Dental Technician Week in Oklahoma. Margaret Beth Riley was a young dental technician from Weatherford who had lost her life in a Colorado skiing accident. Then came the thirty-four members of the Northwest Central State College glee club, The Stemwinders, for me to send them off on a concert tour to Peru, Argentina and Bolivia. I signed a document making them official Oklahoma Is OK Goodwill Ambassadors. They showed their appreciation by singing a cappella "The Surrey with the Fringe on Top" and "Poor Jud" from *Oklahoma!*

That made me think all the more about the Russian spy at the JackieMart–Utoka.

I called the OBI office, and officially and formally told them to contact C. and tell him that, I, the acting governor, wanted to talk to him immediately.

In less than five minutes, Janice Alice informed me C. was on the line. I went through some preliminaries, including a short, light report on my day's activities with the dental technicians and the Crime and Penal Commission.

He said he had just received some preliminary information by phone report on the grease pirates. "The Oklahoma City PD plans to take care of them tonight," he said. "They'll never bother Tommy Walt or anyone else again."

I thanked him and then said: "What's the plan for the Sooner Spy? There's something about it all that bothers me, C."

"Forget it, Mack. I just can't say a thing about it. It's no longer in our bailiwick."

"Forget it, nothing, Mr. Director. It is very much in *my* bailiwick. I am the governor of this state today and you serve at the pleasure of the governor, please remember."

"You firing me?"

"Just reminding you that this is not a personal question. Now let me repeat it: What is the plan for the Sooner Spy?"

"Please don't ask me. Please don't. I gave my word to Colley."

"Do you ever look at the check you get every month?"

"Sure . . ."

"You ever remember seeing Collins's signature on it?"

"Mack, please. This is highly secret, supersensitive stuff between law enforcement professionals. As you know, Colley's already down on me for telling you about this guy in the first place. Trust is everything in my business."

"It is in mine too, C. They call it the public trust, in fact. The people of Oklahoma trust me to protect them from enemies foreign and domestic. And that includes Russian assassins. They trust me to make sure the head of the OBI does his job...."

"I *am* doing my job, damn it, Mack. You have to trust *me.*"

I cleared my throat a couple of times into the phone. And breathed loudly enough to be heard in Utoka.

"Mack, I don't know much, and what I do know I cannot tell you. There are some things not even acting governors are permitted to know."

"I hereby order you to tell me what you know."

Now it was C. who cleared his throat and breathed.

"I hereby refuse to comply with your order."

"I really should fire you, you know."

"I'll call The Chip in Japan and cry."

"I hope your other ear falls off."

"Same to your good eye."

I hung up the phone, and my one eye fell to the large leather-bound appointment book Jackie had given me for Christmas—she gave me a new one every year. This was Wednesday. Tomorrow was Thursday. Rotary Day. In Oklahoma City.

And in Utoka.

I had Janice Alice get Bill Hagood on the phone.

First I told him that his Put Oklahoma Towns on the Globe Week was an excellent idea and that if he would draft something I would be delighted to have it written up officially and sign it. Then I said it turned out I was going to be in his neighborhood the next day and would be available to speak to Rotary if he wanted. He jumped at it. Of course. I *was* the acting governor, after all. He said it would be no problem to reschedule the scheduled speakers, a Nazarene minister and his wife from Phillips, Oklahoma, who had just returned from India and China with slides and stories.

He said it would be the first time in history that a governor, acting or real, had addressed the Rotary Club of Utoka.

He said he was glad he had always voted for me.

Despite the uncertainty and peril of my trip, the next morning I left Oklahoma City for Utoka a happy man. Tommy Walt had called in the middle of the night. Staked-out policemen in dirty, greasy plain clothes had apprehended the grease pirates and made restaurant grease collection safe for the honest businessman. "I'm going to make it, Dad. I really am. I've got a real helper now. A young psychology major from OU who likes to get dirty. I might buy another truck and expand. Maybe do some merging, even." Jackie raised her glass of orange juice at the breakfast table to "Oklahoma's beloved Father of the Year."

C. was waiting for me at the Utoka airport; like a border patrolman trying to keep an undesirable illegal alien from entering. I knew he'd be there. The highway patrol had to arrange for a car and driver to meet my plane. The OBI was routinely informed of the movements of the governor, even if he was the acting governor. I was already scheduled to dedicate a new tourist attraction outside Sturant in the afternoon, but I did not tell Janice Alice to alter the arrangements for an earlier Utoka stop until after nine in the morning. We were wheels-up in the governor's six-seat Beechcraft Executive two hours later.

"I have come to speak to my fellow Rotarians of Utoka," I said to C. "Routine."

"Forget it, Mack," he said. "Until late yesterday afternoon some preacher and his wife were set to talk to your fellow Rotarians of Utoka about how they say 'Jesus' in Chinese."

We were behind the closed doors of the airport administrator's office, the same place where I had looked at FBI and CIA picture albums for Calvin Howell Youngfoot.

"What are you up to, Mack?"

"Nothing."

"This thing is almost over here. Your young KGB man got here early this morning. We're with him like his shadow and soul. He will probably make his move soon. Don't blow it for us."

"What's 'it,' C.?"

"The plan."

"What plan?"

"It's Collins and his people's. I don't know that much about it myself. Everything is *need* to know."

"I need to know, C. I am the governor of this state this day and what is happening here in Utoka this day is something I need to know about."

"Please, Mack. Please get back on that plane and get the hell out of here."

"Sorry. I made a commitment to be here today, and I keep my commitments."

"Mack, don't put me in a position to . . . Well, our friendship means a lot to me. We've been through a lot together."

"What's this got to do with our friendship?"

"Things can and could happen. . . ."

"I smell a rat, C. Something's going on here with this 'plan' that just does not add up. But relax. I'm just here to make a speech to the Rotary Club."

"Mack, there are no rats to smell. Please remember Colley and I are the good guys. We're on America's side. Oklahoma's side. *Your* side."

"I'm late for my speech," I said. I left the office, and went outside, got in a black trooper-driven car and told the driver to take me to the Best Western–Utoka Inn.

Bill Hagood took me directly to the head table. There was always a chance the Sooner Spy would not be there. But unless Calvin made his move or some other calamity fell before the twelve-noon meeting time, I knew he would come. He was the president of the club. Death is about the only excuse good enough for a Rotary president to miss a meeting.

And there he was. Alive, smiling, taking a gulp of iced tea. We arrived at the head table and I went right over to him. He put down his tea, jumped to his feet and stuck out his hand.

"Governor, it is so good to see you again," he said. "This is such a special treat to have you come here today." The tension from our encounter the week before was gone. He appeared completely relaxed, as if he did not know a KGB assassin was in town right then plotting his murder.

"Good to see you," I said. "How is life at the JackieMart?"

"Excellent. Perfect. I love my JackieMart. I love the opportunity your wife has created for me and others like me. Please pass on my thank you. I should have said that when you were here last week. But I didn't and I am sorry. You were in such a hurry...."

"I will tell her. She will be so pleased."

We shook hands again.

"I look forward to your speech," he said.

I followed Bill Hagood to the other side of the speaker's rostrum, where I was to sit, right there next to Bill so we could talk about globes and other matters of importance.

An awful feeling came over me as I walked away from the Sooner Spy—a feeling of dread. As on the afternoon when I was twelve, when my dad picked up my mother in his arms and drove her to the hospital, before she died of the burst appendix.

I was brought lunch this time. It was mock drumsticks, broccoli with a cheese sauce and two boiled new potatoes. Plus a hard roll, a pat of margarine and a tossed salad with Thousand Island dressing. Plus iced tea and rice pudding.

Bill then talked. And talked. He thanked me profusely for agreeing to declare Put Oklahoma Towns on the Globe Week in Oklahoma. He said a lot of people in the club had laughed at his idea at first but they were coming around. He said people who sat around and waited for good things to happen often ended up with no things at all. It had a Buffalo Joe ring to it.

Then it came time to talk to the man on my left. He said his name was Sanders. Hastings John Sanders. He said he was the editor and publisher of the *Utoka Caller-Times* and he wondered if I minded if he asked me a few questions about public service. I said fine. He asked me if I liked being the acting governor more than I liked being just lieutenant governor. I told him that all I wanted to do was to serve the people of Oklahoma. The function of that service was up to the people. He said he was really glad to hear that, because he did not believe that was the attitude of most politicians anymore. Anymore? I said. Yes, sir, he said, being in public office used to mean being in public service. No more. Now it means being in service to yourself. Helping yourself. I said it sounded to me as if he had had a sour experience with some public servant. True, he said. With all of them. Not about stealing money. That's to be expected. Fine. No problem. It's stealing the truth and thus insulting the people's intelligence he was sick of. Stealing the truth? Yes, sir. Lying. I watch those presidents and senators and congressmen and secretaries of state, defense and so on on television, and you do not have to be God or a polygraph to know when they're lying. Not on the big things. The little ones. The medium-sized ones. The ones nobody cares about. Like, let's say one of our Sooner senators in Washington votes for a bill that helps the oil boys in Bartlesville or Ponca City get around a tax problem. The senator does not say he did it to help the Oklahoma oil people. No, sir. He says he did it for the good of America. Now everybody knows he's lying through his teeth. Everybody just smiles and says fine. Same things happens when the secretary of defense or some other so on says he'll never compromise on killing some big-deal weapons system. But he always does. And everybody knows it when he says it. But everybody just smiles and says fine. Same thing when the president stands there at a press conference on television and says he didn't mean it when he called Russia a bunch of Commie thugs. Everybody knows he meant it. But everybody just smiles and says fine. It's one thing to turn the other way when politicians steal. It's another to do it when they lie. And if you do it on the little and the medium-sized lies, then someday they'll be tempted to try it on the big ones. That's what worries me. We're getting so we expect our politicians to lie to us. Someday we're going to be sorry. Someday. What do you think?

I told him I had never thought about that before.

I turned back to Bill Hagood. "How did you happen to go into banking?" I asked.

He said: "When I was in the ninth grade in the small town in Ohio where I grew up, our homeroom teacher said one morning that the bank her uncle worked at was looking for kids to come in on Saturday morning and roll pennies, nickels, dimes and other coins. At the end of the week they always had drawers of them and the regular employees just did not have the time to roll them. She said the bank would pay ten cents for each roll rolled. It seemed like a good thing to do. So I went down there that next Saturday morning. I took to it like honey to a rib. I loved counting out those coins and stacking them and touching them and smelling them and talking about them. I was also good. I could roll twice as many rolls as anyone else. It was a natural for me. Coins, money, banking was a natural for me. So I decided to be a banker. On the fourth Saturday, I came home from the bank and told my daddy I was going to be president of a bank someday. After college I did some other things first, but eventually I landed here with the First National Bank of Utoka. Now I'm the president."

It suddenly became dead certain to me that Bill Hagood was the CIA's Utoka contact Collins had talked about.

"What did you do before you came here?" I asked.

"Nothing much to speak of," he said.

The Sooner Spy brought the meeting to order. We had the invocation and the Pledge of Allegiance and sang "God Bless America." Visiting Rotarians were introduced. Then came announcements and reports.

Bill Hagood went to the podium and updated the membership on the Globe Project. Responses were beginning to come in, he said. North American Map and Globe in Worcester, Massachusetts, had agreed to consider putting Utoka on its next globe that was large enough to accommodate towns of Utoka's size. That's progress, Bill said. Kansas City Globes, Inc., a major maker of plastic blow-up globes, had also agreed to consider Utoka seriously for one of its summer pool-floater models. Bill urged everyone to come alive on carrying out individual assignments. "Write those letters and make those calls," he said. "Utoka's future is in putting Utoka on the globe."

The Sooner Spy followed Bill with his own personal endorsement of the project, reminding his fellow Rotarians of the Rotary motto, "Service Above Self."

The treasurer reported the club to be in pretty good shape. The chairman of the membership committee offered the names of three new members, who were introduced and voted in. The community service committee chairman reminded everyone that volunteers were still needed for this Saturday's picnic for the kids at the state retardation center outside of town. He asked for a show of hands and got ten or twelve just like that.

Another committee chairman reminded everybody of the weekend auditions for parts in the upcoming production of *Oklahoma!* to raise money for new high school band uniforms. It seemed to me a natural for the Sooner Spy to sing a part, and I hoped he would still be alive and around for it.

Then it was time to introduce me. Bill Hagood went back to the microphone.

He said I had overcome my early unfortunate beginnings in Kansas, where I had had the bad luck to be born. He said I had entered politics at an early age in Adabel, and was the youngest elected county commissioner in the history of Oklahoma. He said I was an excellent lieutenant governor and was, in fact, now the acting governor in the absence of the real governor, so if anyone had any uncles or whatever in jail who needed pardons, this was the time to ask. He said I was married to the famous founder and president of JackieMarts Inc. and that we had four children. He said I was a loyal member of the Downtown Rotary in Oklahoma City, having first joined Rotary when I was in Adabel. He said I was known statewide for my wit and honesty. But soon I would be better known for being the man who proclaimed Put Oklahoma Towns on the Globe Week in Oklahoma. That drew a big applause.

He did not say anything about the black patch over my left eye. Nobody ever did in introductions. Out of politeness. But it was the one thing everybody in every audience was dying to know about. How did he lose that eye? Was it shot out in a war? Was it poked out in a fight? Did he trip and fall on a stick or a sword? Did lightning strike it out? What happened, for God's sake? Why does he wear that black patch, for God's sake? They make glass eyes that look almost real, for God's sake!

I thanked Bill for his kind introduction and said: "The

one thing Bill did not point out is that I am the first one-eyed acting governor in the history of Oklahoma. Just like I was the first one-eyed lieutenant governor and the first one-eyed county commissioner. Now it's possible y'all may have already noticed that—you being smart Rotarians like you are."

They laughed.

"Now I also know there are those among you who are wondering about what happened to the other eye. But you were too polite to ask. And I appreciate that kind of Rotarian thoughtfulness and courtesy. But I'm not the least bit sensitive about it. I don't mind telling you the whole story. I don't mind your knowing that I went into politics only after I couldn't make it as a pirate. It was a natural move. Both pirates and politicians should wear patches because their work is so similar. Both rob the rich to pay the poor."

It brought down the house. Wit and honesty always did.

And I went on to say a few words about the need for holding the line on state spending; for repaving our farm-to-market roads; for doubling the size of our state vocational education system; for ridding our state of dirty books and movies and eliminating drugs and auto theft from our Sooner cities and towns; for bringing new jobs and industry to Oklahoma; for guaranteeing all Oklahomans, of every race, sex, creed and color, an opportunity for education and occupation commensurate with their abilities. *Commensurate* means equal: equal to their smartness.

I was careful what I said. I did not want Hastings Sanders jumping up from his chair and yelling "Lie!" every two or three minutes.

And I had an idea. A crazy idea. A Buffalo Joe kind of

idea. I had not come to Utoka with anything in mind to do, really. I had come just to be here when whatever happened happened.

I was talking humbly about the honor it was for me to serve as acting governor for these eleven days of Oklahoma history. And I said: "One of the most glorious things I get to do as acting governor is to go around this state and see its many tourist attractions. I have always believed that Oklahoma is the Great Undiscovered State of the fifty states. One day we are going to get discovered and then we're not going to be able to stir the tourists in cars and tour buses with a stick. It's going to be bumper to bumper from Vinita and Broken Bow on the east to Boise City and Hollis on the west. They're going to be crowding our interstates and state highways, our boulevards and bike paths. And those crowds of people from out of state—from New York and Minnesota, from Florida and Wyoming, from Vermont and California, and, yes, from Texas and maybe even Arkansas—are going to bring as much money in here as God did when he put oil under our fertile soil."

I was interrupted with applause. Applause of hope.

"This very afternoon I am having the extreme pleasure of dedicating still another major attraction. T. Whitfield and Sarah Davidson's One-of-a-Kind Roadside Sculpture Park. I am sure y'all have read all about it. . . ."

I scanned the audience for pairs of eyes that had read all about it. Ten or twelve. Not bad.

"It's outside Sturant. In a pasture. The finest collection of outdoor advertising sculpture ever assembled in one place in the world. People will come from the world over to see it in that one place called Oklahoma. When I leave here in a few minutes I will be flying right there for the dedication ceremony. And you know something, I just had an idea."

I looked down the head table at the Sooner Spy. "Why don't I take your president, Art Pennington, with me? What about it, Art? I'll have you back home by dark. Go with me and represent Rotary and Utoka. What about it, Art?"

"Go, Art!" his fellow Rotarians yelled. "Yeah, Art! Go! Yeah, yeah, yeah."

Bill Hagood was the only one not yelling. His well-tanned face had turned gray. Like C.'s.

· 11 ·

Sunshine and
Opportunity

"SOME PEOPLE call it Junk. Some people call it Nothing.
Sarah and I call it Art," said T. Whitfield Davidson.

"Sarah is the one who calls it Nothing," said Sarah Davidson. "Whit is the only one who calls it Art."

We were in the Davidsons' white Lincoln Continental convertible. Whit was driving and Sarah was in the front passenger seat. The Sooner Spy and I were in the back. We were on a pre–ribbon-cutting private tour of T. Whitfield and Sarah Davidson's One-of-a-Kind Roadside Sculpture Park.

Whit was in his late sixties. He had made his money in the quick-copy business. He was among the first to realize that a man with a Xerox machine and a lot of paper could make a lot of money making copies of things for other people. He now had wholly owned or franchised Fast Copy

Heavens in twenty-four states, including his first in Ard-
more, Oklahoma, and three foreign countries. Sarah was
one of those forty-year-old blondes who wish they were
twenty-five-year-old blondes. Both were tanned and dressed
like golf pros at a country club in Tulsa.

There were forty-seven pieces in the collection. They were
set along both sides of a private blacktop road that went
through a grass pasture next to the Davidsons' place, the
Double D Ranch, off State Highway 99. The road was twelve
miles long from the opening gate to the exit gate.

"Plenty of room to keep expanding the collection," Whit
explained.

"Over your dead body," Sarah responded.

Just inside the gate was Sculpture One. It was a double-
life-sized painted steel-plated statue of Gordon MacRae playing Curly in *Oklahoma!* Gordon had his hat between his
hands over his stomach. His head was to the sky. Whit said
the statue had stood for years on a county road outside Enid
advertising Curly's, a drive-in restaurant that didn't make
it.

I looked at the Sooner Spy, who was smiling. Obviously
because of his own special ties to *Oklahoma!*

Sculpture Two was an Orange Crush bottle, ten feet high.
"Got it from a bottler in Abilene, Kansas," said Whit.

"Ike's hometown," I said, trying to make conversation.

"Ike Eisenhower," Art said, trying to remain a part of
the conversation. The KGB had taught him some American
history.

We got out of the car and went over to the bottle. I felt
it. It was made of tin.

"It had been out in front of this guy's bottling plant for

forty years," Whit explained. "He sold it to me for a song."

We walked down and across the road to a giant paint can that was lying on its side with light blue paint spilling out into a puddle. All fake, of course. "Got it off the top of a paint store in Jackson, Tennessee," Whit explained.

"Look at that next one," he said with the pride of a boy who had a new red wagon or something. The next one was a perfectly sculpted huge golden hand with the forefinger pointing to the sky. To heaven. "It was on top of a Methodist church south of Vicksburg, Mississippi. The wind blew it off and I bought it. Look at it!" I looked at it all right. And concluded that it must have really been strange to drive down an innocent Mississippi highway and suddenly come across a huge gold finger sticking up in the air.

We moved on to admire a steel Borden cow. A huge model of an orange Allied Van Lines truck and trailer. A wooden vanilla soft-ice-cream cone from a drive-in in Asheville, North Carolina. A fifteen-foot-high golf club from a miniature golf place in Alamogordo, New Mexico. A house-sized chicken with a golf club under a wing and a golf cap on its head from a St. Joseph, Missouri, restaurant called Chicken in the Rough. Giant replicas of my friend Colonel Sanders in his white suit and Big Boy in his red-checkered overalls and black cowlicked hair with a tray of hamburgers. A monstrous Pepsi-Cola bottle top. A black and white dog listening to an old-fashioned RCA phonograph. A pig with wings from The Flying Pig, a South Carolina barbecue place. And a lot of other things like that.

The piece special to me was near the end. It was a stunning, spectacular plaster of Paris replica of Roy Rogers on Trigger. Whit said it had come from in front of a western clothing and memorabilia store outside Victoria, Texas. Trigger was reared back on two legs. Roy, King of the Cowboys, held the reins with his left hand, his cowboy hat in his right. He was smiling, and close up he really did resemble Harvey Gaines in that open Gainesville casket. Or really the other way around. Roy Rogers was special because he had played a part in changing my life. He and Dale Evans, Gabby Hayes and Trigger had come to Adabel to make a movie when I was a young man. They did a little show for the town before they left and I was lucky enough to get called up on the stage. I performed pretty well just talking to Roy and it was mostly because of that that I was elected county commissioner. And that led to my becoming lieutenant governor and now, for eleven days, acting governor.

The last sculpture was what Whit called his pride and joy. It was a her. A woman. She stood more than twenty feet high and was made out of thin steel. Her hair was cut a lot like Jacqueline Kennedy's. She was in a short skirt that came just above her knees and was painted green, a short-sleeved blouse that was painted yellow, and purple open-toed high-heel shoes. Her face was made up but not for going out on the town—just to the store to get some milk or to school to pick up her kid. Her right hand and arm were raised up and away from her body; her left hand and arm were tight, down her other side.

"She came from a Chrysler-Plymouth dealership in Louisiana," Whit explained. "It's the dealer's wife. She died, her husband sold the dealership and remarried, and I got this. Paid fifteen hundred for it. But it's priceless. Have you ever seen anything like it anywhere, Governor?"

"No," I replied.

The Sooner Spy and I walked up to her. And around her. It was a strange feeling, like checking out a gorgeous Mrs. Gulliver. Or Miss Goliath. I was embarrassed to find myself automatically glancing upward, up her skirt. There wasn't anything to see, of course, just painted metal. I noticed that the Sooner Spy did the same thing. She seemed too real, too alive. No red-blooded American man could resist. Neither could a red-blooded Russian man.

Back in the car, Sarah Davidson said, "She's Whit's sex object. I think he loves her more than he does me."

"She's too big even for me," Whit said.

We all laughed.

Whit drove the white Lincoln Continental convertible back to the main entrance gate, where a couple hundred people had gathered in front of a small stage for my speech and the rest of the opening ceremonies.

A high school band from Sturant played a medley of appropriate songs, most of them themes from movies and musicals. Whit welcomed everyone and then introduced me.

I spoke to the crowd of the gift T. Whitfield and Sarah Davidson were making to the people of Oklahoma. A gift not only of objects but also of their vision, a vision that saw art in these commonplace objects of our roadside life.

"Someday, when the history of our particular time on this earth is written, there will be a few words about Whit and Sarah," I said. "They will say Whit and Sarah were the art anthropologists of their time, finding, admiring and preserving the artifacts that made up an accurate record of the roadside life of the American people."

Then I had another idea. Again, just standing there talking.

I looked over at the Sooner Spy, who was sitting in a

folding chair on the stage next to Sarah Davidson. I said to the audience: "I would like to introduce a man who came with me on this special occasion. He is Art Pennington, president of the Rotary Club in Utoka. Art, please stand up and take a bow."

The crowd applauded with some hesitancy. They clearly had no idea why they were clapping for the president of the Utoka Rotary Club or why he was taking a bow.

"What you may not know about Art is that he has a secret life."

Art's face turned from rosy Oklahoma red to snowy Minnesota white.

"He also knows and sings all of the words from *Oklahoma!*" I turned to the band, which was sitting in white and blue uniforms in chairs off to my left. "How about 'Oh, What a Beautiful Mornin'"?"

The band director leaped into action. The Sooner Spy, color still not returned to his face, came to the microphone. He had no choice.

There was a chord and then from the mouth of the former KGB station chief in Washington came the words: "There's a bright haze on the shadow ... Oh, what a beautiful mornin' ... Oh, what a beautiful evening ..."

He looked at me with a cry of help on his face. "I don't know the words or the music," he said. "I really don't." He smiled and bowed toward the puzzled audience and returned to his seat.

But the band kept playing and the leader motioned for all of us to stand and join in singing the chorus. Two hundred of us Sooners there on our Oklahoma prairie raised our voices together. This time to sing it right.

"Oh, what a beautiful mornin',
Oh, what a beautiful day,
I got a beautiful feeling,
Everything's going my way."

As the little Beechcraft lifted off the blacktop runway outside Sturant I knew this was it. The time had come for me to decide what exactly I was already doing and what I was going to do next. And exactly why.

Art and I had not talked much on the flight over. It took only forty-five minutes and we discussed mostly Rotary and the wonders of JackieMart. Now we had to talk about spies and assassins—after I first apologized for humiliating him in front of all those people.

"I would have sworn somebody told me you were an expert on *Oklahoma!*," I said.

"I am not good with music," he said, and that was that.

I asked him, "Where do you come from originally?"

"Michigan," he said, as automatically as if it were true. "A place called Schoolcraft. South of Kalamazoo."

"I knew from your accent it couldn't be Oklahoma," I said.

"I was born in Hungary. I came to Michigan with my family after the uprising."

"What did your father do?"

"He was a machinist."

"How did you happen to come to our Sooner State?"

"I wanted more sunshine and opportunity."

More sunshine and opportunity. It sounded like an Oklahoma Business and Industry Development Commission slogan. Come to Oklahoma, where there's more sunshine and opportunity and the wind comes sweeping down the plain and there are nothing but beautiful mornings.

"How do you like being an American?" I said.

"It has been my salvation as a person," he said automatically, as if it were true.

"How do you like being a Rotarian?"

"It is my favorite thing to be. Why are you asking me all of these questions?"

"Friendliness. Basic friendliness. I am interested in people. Where they come from, how they got where they are..."

"Governor, I am afraid there is something you want to tell me."

I leaned forward. And prepared to lower my voice. The plane's two engines made plenty of noise, but I knew enough about C. and his taping abilities to be careful.

"Well, yes, I do have something to say...."

Then, at that precise moment, a providence called Oklahoma weather intervened.

The little plane started jumping and lurching. I looked outside. The sky was a churning black and gray. There were flashes of lightning way out there. And the roar of thunder.

The copilot crawled out of the cockpit to say:

"We can't get near Utoka right now, Governor. We're going to swing around this weather and wait it out in Adabel. They're clear as a bell over there. Sorry. We've notified Oklahoma City and the highway patrol."

It was another of those blessings and glories that had come my way since I lost my left eye.

Two uniformed highway patrolmen were at the Adabel airport when we landed. They said their orders were to stand ready to do all that needed to be done to maintain my safety and comfort until we took off again. They also had a message. It was to call OBI director Hayes at a number in Utoka. They said the message was Code Silver, which I had never heard of. They said it was second in gravity only to Code Platinum, which meant "evacuate the state because of nuclear attack from the sky or a massive invasion on the ground." From Arkansas?

They escorted the Sooner Spy to a seat in a small waiting room and then ushered me into an airport manager's office. It had framed eight-by-ten color photographs of civilian and military planes on the walls, and on the desk were five or six ashtrays with little metal propellers on them.

C. came on the phone less than Code Silver. I had to listen very carefully at first to the pitch and the punctuation to get how really angry and upset and Code Silver he was.

"Kidnapping is a federal offense, Mack," C. said. "Kidnapping a president of a local Rotary Club is a capital federal offense. Your head may roll over this."

"That would make me the first one-eyed acting governor in Oklahoma history to be beheaded," I replied.

"Mack, don't make me do something stupid to keep you from doing something stupid," he said. "Something else stupid, I should say."

"It's not my fault a thunderstorm hit Utoka."

"It'll be clearing here soon. This is an awful thing you've done, Mack. Why did you shanghai him to Sturant? What are you up to?"

"It was an impulse thing. I was going over there for a sculpture-garden dedication and thought he might get a kick out of going with me. He had a great time. I even prevailed on him to sing 'Oh, What a Beautiful Mornin'' for the crowd at the dedication. You should have been there. . . ."

"You got him to sing? Jesus, Mack. Jesus! Have you said anything to him about what you know? Does he know about . . . you know, the young guy?"

"You mean, you know, the young guy who has come to murder him? He hasn't heard it from me if he knows. I have said nothing to him about that. Not yet."

"Mack, no! Don't!"

"You can't order me around."

"Don't be so sure."

He breathed into the telephone like an obscene phone caller.

Then I knew for sure that the Utoka Sparrow had discovered his old Thunderbird sign missing from that closet.

I also knew then for sure that providence had diverted me to Adabel for a reason. This was where I could find and consult the Second Son of God, the man Jackie and I, among others, called Brother Walt. He was pastor of the First Church of the Holy Road, and he was the large wonderful human being who took Jackie, Pepper and me into his life when we first came to Adabel and who guided us to our respective destinies. He was also the smartest person in Oklahoma, if not the whole world. I mean smart smart: kitchen and alley smart as well as front-parlor smart. I had turned to him when two and two no longer added up to four or anything else.

Like right now.

I told the Sooner Spy that this was my old hometown and I had to run a quick personal errand while we waited.

I hoped he didn't mind. He said he would be fine. There were plenty of magazines to read at the airport, and he grabbed a copy of *U.S. News & World Report.*

I asked the highway patrolmen to take me to the First Church of the Holy Road as fast as their car would operate. Pulling up in front of the church, sirens and red lights going, was a perfect way to pay a call on the Second Son of God.

But he wasn't there. His secretary, Ida Henderson, hugged me and said he was over at Channel 42, Adabel's only TV station. She said he was auditioning.

"Auditioning for what?"

"To be one of those TV evangelists. A couple of men from Dallas called and then they came by and then they called again and came back...."

I ran out of the church and back to the police car. I gave the patrolmen the address of Channel 42 and said speed was still essential. And this time I meant it.

I found Brother Walt in a TV studio that was small and empty except for him, two cameras and two cameramen, a shiny waxed floor and rows of lights on the ceiling. He was standing in front of one of the cameras with a microphone in his hand. He was preaching. With feeling.

"I ask you, brothers and sisters out there. I ask you now. Have you found The Way? Are you on the road to Glory? Have you found that God is Great? God *is* Great...."

"Cut!"

It was a voice coming out of a loudspeaker, a male voice.

"Thank you, Reverend. But we still don't quite have it. Remember, it's not really a TV camera you are preaching to. Those are people out there behind the red light. Imagine the face of your favorite person, your most receptive church member. Or somebody. Also, on using the microphone: Remember, it is an active participant in the message. Use it to hammer at points. Bring it right up to your lips and breathe into it. Snap your fingers into it. Use it like it is a part of you. . . ."

"Cut!" I yelled. And I stepped from the back of the studio so Brother Walt could see me.

"Mack, the leader of the free world of Oklahoma. God is Great if it isn't you."

He then said, into his microphone, "The distinguished lieutenant governor of Oklahoma has dropped in to see me, gentlemen. Could we take a break?"

"We're paying top dollar for this studio, Reverend," said the voice on the loudspeaker system.

"Tell them I am the acting *governor* right now. For eleven days. And if they do not allow me to talk to you, I will order this place raided and them arrested on charges of indecency and contributing to the delinquency of an elderly Holy Road preacher. . . ."

"Elderly?" Then he said into the active participating microphone: "He's the acting governor for eleven days."

There was a pause while the voice on the loudspeaker obviously consulted with somebody else.

"All right, then. In honor of the acting governor. Crew, take five," said the voice a moment later.

Brother Walt grabbed me by the shoulders. And hugged me. I loved him. He loved me, too, but not as much as he used to. He was partial to sinners, the worse the better. People who did only good things were of small interest to him because they had only a small need of him. He was originally attracted to Pepper, Jackie and me years ago because we were down-and-out and bad—particularly Pepper, who had several warrants out for his arrest. The crimes were mostly minor, though, and they were all dismissed in exchange for his agreeing to go into the Marines. So he could fall on a hand grenade and die.

"What is this all about?" I asked Brother Walt. I could not disguise my agitation.

He picked up on it. Immediately. And loved it. He had a way of playing, of lowering his voice as if to say, "Now, listen up, what you are about to hear is the closest you'll ever get to hearing the Voice of God." He did it now and said: "Well, now, my concerned friend, what this is all about is Glory. Putting lights and cameras on the road to Glory. The Holy Road. The Road that I follow and the Road, I hope, that you still follow . . ."

"Seriously, Walt. What is going on?"

I guess he could see that I was at least trying to will away my agitation. There was nothing he enjoyed more than taking on people who were agitated with him.

He grinned and slapped my shoulders again. "Okay Mr. Acting Governor, here is the word: Two smiling young men in tan suits with vests and shellacked brown-and-white shoes and perfume under their arms came in to see me a few weeks ago. They said they ran Word Communications Incorporated in Dallas. They said the evangelical future was in Christian television. They said the day was here for spreading the Word of God with pictures and sound. For speaking and converting millions instead of dozens and hundreds. They said it wasn't too much to predict that eventually there will be no churches the way we know them now. People will still gather on Sunday morning but not to hear their local pastor, but to watch and hear a Master National Preacher on big-screen television. Like they do in Los Angeles and New York now for watching championship boxing matches on closed-circuit TV. They said they were scouring the country for those Master National Preachers now. They said they were pleased to tell me I was on the list. They said they had heard about me from everybody everywhere. They said I was really good. They said they had already checked me out. Quietly. Secretly. Just showing up on Sunday morning for my sermons three or four times. Coming and then leaving unannounced. They were now prepared to take the Big Step."

We had walked over to a corner of the studio. There were two metal folding chairs there. We sat down.

He continued: "Mack, they wanted to give me an audition. They said some people do well in the pulpit in the flesh but just can't project on television. A lot of people in politics have that problem. Lyndon Johnson did. There's a knack to it. Some say it's either there naturally or it isn't. They said they couldn't take any chances, so they wondered if I minded coming to Dallas for an audition session. On a private plane with all expenses paid, of course. They talked a lot about expenses. About money. About this was where it was going to be in the Christian future. In preaching on television. Did I want to be a part of this future? Did I want to have my word along with God's word spread to the entire United States of America? To the whole world eventually? Did I want to be recognized in Pizza Huts and 7-Eleven stores? Did I want to be a second Billy Graham?"

"Why didn't you tell them to buzz off? You're a preacher, not a TV actor...."

"I told them I did not go on private planes to Dallas. They said, Fine, then what about doing it in a studio in Adabel? I said, No harm in that. So they set it up.

"And that is what is going on here, Mack. How are your wonder woman Jackie and the kids doing?"

"Walt, you cannot do this."

"Mack, I can if I want to and Jesus approves."

"That's crazy."

"Any crazier than you being lieutenant governor of Oklahoma?"

"I can't let you do this."

"Sorry, but it's not something the lieutenant governor or even the acting governor of Oklahoma lets or does not let me do."

He started to stand up. I motioned for him to stay seated.

"I'm in trouble, Walt. I need your help. That's why I'm really here."

"Trouble? You're in trouble?" His face broke into a happy grin. "Well, Glory. God is Great. Tell me all that you have done, Mack."

I told him about the Sooner Spy. The whole story. How I had exposed the man's new identity and location to a KGB assassin. How on orders from C. and Collins, I had pointed Calvin the Assassin right to his target in Utoka. How I had come to Utoka and kidnapped the Sooner Spy and taken him to Sturant and how he was sitting out at the Adabel airport reading a copy of *U.S. News & World Report*. I told him that something was up and I did not like it, even though I did not know what it was.

"What do you *think* is up?" he asked me. "I thought C. Hayes was a good man and a good friend of yours."

"He is. But it must be out of his hands. I think the CIA's using the Utoka man as some kind of bait for something. Collins said something to me about fishing. . . ."

"You think they're going to allow Spy Two to murder Spy One, is that it? Is that what it all comes down to?"

"Yes, sir."

"You said the guy came over to our side. Why would we want the Russians to kill him?"

"I have no idea. . . ."

"Reverend?" It was the voice on the loudspeaker. "Time to get started again. We need to run through the healing bits."

I stared at Brother Walt, the Second Son of God, the Smartest Man in Oklahoma. I rendered unto him the nastiest, most outrageous look of indignation and surprise I could manage.

"The healing bits?" I said with scorn and sarcasm. "Are you going to ask the audience to put their lame and broken limbs, their cancerous and TB-ravaged bodies, their diseased and dying children right there on top of their TV sets?"

Brother Walt stood up.

He said: "You're right, Mack. Let's get out of here."

"God is Great," I said.

"I can do without being recognized in Pizza Huts and 7-Elevens," he said as we walked out the front door of the TV station.

We turned to the left and started north up the sidewalk toward downtown, toward the First Church of the Holy Road. I motioned to the two troopers to follow us in the car.

"Now where were we with your terrible, terrible problem?" said Walt.

"We were wondering why *we*, the United States of America, would want to help the Russians kill one of our own spies."

"Well, clearly we cannot figure that out. I take it you do *not* want this Sooner Spy, as you call him, harmed."

"He's the president of the Utoka Rotary."

"Over at the Lions they would say that was reason enough to harm him. But hold on awhile longer if you do not mind."

"Hold on?"

"I need a few more seconds to completely swallow and digest the idea of a defected Russian spy being president of the Rotary Club in Utoka, Oklahoma."

We went past the courthouse. Past the four statues to the war dead there, all in a row. For the Spanish-American, World War I, World War II and the Korean War. The statues for the Spanish-American War and the Korean War had been built by me when I was county commissioner. The sculptor had used Pepper as the model for the Korean War statue, a life-sized bronze replica of a U.S. Marine. Pepper was already dead and we'd had no photographs of him, so it wasn't easy. Close up, the statue's face resembled mine more than Pepper's but nobody had noticed.

I wondered if they had started thinking about a statue for the Vietnam War dead. There was a large green lawn with plenty of room for many more statues from many more wars.

I glanced up at my old office window. I'd spent many hours standing there looking down at the statues and at the lawn and at Adabel, Oklahoma.

"There are choices," Walt said. "The First Choice is to go out to the airport and inform your Sooner Spy friend that you know who he is and that you think he's been set

163

up. Ask him how he likes that, and if he thinks that is a bad idea, then offer him the services of the State of Oklahoma in helping him."

"I thought about that. In fact, I was about to do it when we got diverted here. That seems so unfair to C. and the CIA. I may be wrong about what they're up to. Everybody is already upset with me for what I have already done. . . ."

"The Second Choice is to do nothing. Deposit this man back in Utoka and fly away to continue your eleven-day reign as acting governor of Oklahoma. Put it behind you as somebody else's business."

"I can't do that, Walt. I just can't."

"The Third Choice is direct action. Take him back to Utoka, go to C. and the CIA man, and demand to know what is going on. Bark some orders as governor. Throw your weight around. And you make it as clear as Arkansas spring water that either they do what you say or you fire C. and go public about the CIA."

So I told him about the old Thunderbird sign. I had to.

He went into a state of Glory. He was enraptured with the idea that I, the sweet and wonderful One-Eyed Mack, Oklahoma's pleasant and much-loved first one-eyed lieutenant governor and acting governor, had been so overtaken by the devil that I had committed burglary to get a bus depot sign.

He moved swiftly to a dark green wooden bench on the corner of the courthouse lawn. He went to his knees, put his head in his hands for a few silent moments, raised his head. And prayed.

"Dear Lord and Savior, forgive Mack his awfulness. Forgive him for letting the devil take hold of his soul. Forgive him for lusting after a bus depot sign so ferociously that it caused him to break and enter the sanctity of another person's place. Forgive him, dear Lord and Savior, so he may make amends and move on. Forgive him so he can move swiftly now to carry out a dangerous and worthy mission in Your name. A mission that could save the life of one of Your children. A child of godless communism who has seen the light of Glory on the other side. Amen."

He jumped to his feet and grabbed my shoulders once again with his large hands.

"There are times in a man's life that he must take risks. This is one of those times for you. Risk it, Mack."

·12·
Risking It

W<small>E HAD</small> quite a reception committee at the Utoka
airport. C. and Collins and a platoon of men dis-
guised as airplane mechanics, taxi drivers and delivery truck
drivers were there to welcome me, along with another platoon of uniformed state and Utoka police officers. Bill Hagood was on hand to greet us, too. Art said he wanted to
go to the JackieMart to see how things were going and to
pick up his car. Bill said he would be glad to drop him.
That was the least he could do for his friend and Rotary
president, he said.

I told Art not to leave with Bill until I had a chance to
say good-bye. Which was going to be right after I told C.
exactly what I wanted. Which was the same thing he wanted.
To talk. In private. Urgently.

"Nothing happens to my friend Art Pennington while we

talk, is that right?" I said. We had stepped right up by the Beechcraft's right wing. No one else was in hearing distance. "Bill takes him to the JackieMart, but you have him under full observation and protection the whole time? Is that right?"

"Precisely," C. said.

"Precisely what?"

"Precisely what you said."

We walked over to Art and Bill Hagood. The Sooner Spy and I shook hands with great feeling and he thanked me for what he called "a special day in my life." I held him by his right hand and with a few pointless words as long as I could and then watched him drive away in Bill Hagood's green Mercury four-door.

C. was right there by me.

"Mack, if you could join Colley and me in the car over there now . . ."

"Forget it, C. You go tell Collins the two of us are going for a walk."

"Where?"

"Around the runway."

"Mack! Come on now. . . ."

"Do as I say or I'll scream to those Utoka cops over there that you have just tried to sell me a marijuana cigarette."

"They'd never believe it."

"Let's try it and see. Officers! Would you . . ."

"Okay, okay."

C., my friend in gray, walked over to a black car, opened the door and talked to somebody in the backseat. And then he returned to me.

I silently signaled for C. to walk on my right, so my one

good eye would match his one good ear. It was dusk and the rain had helped make things prematurely even darker. But we could see where we were walking. We started out down the pockmarked asphalt runway toward a pair of red lights blinking way down at the other end, a hundred yards or so away.

"First, let me say that everything I say now I am saying as the governor of Oklahoma under all of the powers and responsibilities vested in me under the constitution of Oklahoma. Those powers and responsibilities include those of enforcing the laws of this state. I believe the life of one of the citizens of my state, one Art Pennington of Utoka, is in jeopardy. Since it is against the laws of Oklahoma to take another life, I am stepping in to prevent..."

"Mack, don't do this. I beg of you. Do not do this."

"I am sure you can prevent the taking of this man's life. Under my powers as governor of this state, I hereby order you to do so. Now. Immediately. Whatever wicked and woeful and awful things you and the CIA have cooked up must be halted. Now. Immediately. That is an order."

I glanced around at him. He was looking straight ahead. Like we were marching in a parade. Like we were about to pass a reviewing stand. Like he was way, way off somewhere else. Or wished he was. Or was trying to imagine he was. Like he was very sad. I remembered that this man was my friend, my very good friend. I remembered that he and I had worked together informally on several little private matters and on some very large matters. We always trusted each other.

Without a change in facial expression or a pause in his

step, he pulled a piece of paper from his inside suit coat pocket, unfolded it and handed it to me.

He said it was a copy of a crime incident report from the Utoka Police Department. He said the owner of an insurance office in Utoka had reported the theft of an old Thunderbird Motor Coaches bus depot sign. He said the owner described the sign as "a priceless piece of history."

"I like to look over crime reports from around the state, just to stay up on what's happening," he said. "I was looking through them at the Utoka PD and this one caught my eye."

His voice was ever so quiet. Like a movie star's.

We kept walking toward the blinking red lights.

He said: "You stole that sign, Mr. Acting Governor. I checked out the dates. You were in Utoka on or about the day it was stolen. I am sure that if I were to get a search warrant for your house in Oklahoma City we would turn up that sign somewhere. It is against the laws of this state to break and enter insurance offices and steal old bus depot signs."

Now he pulled out his billfold and removed a small red card. I knew what it was. The Miranda warning card.

"You have the right to remain silent. I hereby warn you that anything you say may be used against you in a court of law. You are entitled to be represented by an attorney."

"This is ridiculous," I said. "I am the acting governor of Oklahoma."

"I know. You are also a felon."

I stopped. He stopped.

"I really would hate to think what public exposure of this

would do to you and Jackie and the kids. Think about it, Mack."

Risk it.

"I *have* thought about it. I do not care. I cannot be threatened. I cannot be blackmailed."

I am sure Collins and maybe half a dozen other assorted agents were watching us through binoculars or infrared devices of some kind or other. I am sure we must have been some puzzle standing there in the middle of that darkening runway. Our noses were not more than a foot apart. I could smell the onions from his Big Mac at lunch.

"I guess you heard about the Oklahoma City PD's cleanup of the grease people?" he said suddenly. It was like old times in the backseat of his Lincoln, lunching over a burger, fries and a chocolate shake.

"Yeah, I heard. Thanks. Tommy Walt's going to do fine now. I just have to find another name for what he does. Restaurant grease collection just does not have the right ring of Oklahoma dignity to it."

He laughed.

We each looked away and then back at each other. My one eye had both of his locked.

"Okay. Okay. What do you have in mind?" he said.

C. had blinked. I had won.

"Yell for Collins to get his CIA butt over here on the double," I said. "I will tell you both what I have in mind for both of you."

God is Great, Brother Walt.

I may have imagined it, but through the dusk I think I saw C. approach the black car making a large circle with his right hand, as if he were swinging some person around in the air by his ear.

* * *

Collins had the fast, leggy walk of a natural athlete. He and C. arrived where I was on the tarmac in much less time than it had originally taken C. and me to walk it.

"Governor," Collins said, shaking my hand, "you've had a busy day...."

There would be no small talk—only my speech. I said:

"Yes, indeed I have. Thank you. Now here is the situation. You and C. have only one chance of avoiding personal and professional disaster. And that is to call off whatever it is you are planning here for Art Pennington. If you do not, as governor of this state I will officially intercede. I will dispose of the KGB assassin in my own way. I will get him out of Utoka and Oklahoma. I will make it possible for Art Pennington to leave Utoka alive. I will make arrangements for him to start one more new life. You will either do as I say or face the consequences. Consequences that will be severe, I am sure. I will leave it to you and your agency, Mr. Collins, to explain to the American people why you would have allowed a KGB assassin to operate freely against a defector who has turned his services to the United States of America in exchange for his safety...."

My eye suddenly caught the headlights of Collins's black car heading down the tarmac toward us. It screeched to a halt right beside us. The driver said, "Code Blue on the radio, Mr. Collins." Code Blue? Was that anything like Oklahoma's own Code Silver? Was nuclear attack or an invasion from Arkansas imminent? Who chooses the colors for all of these codes anyhow? Why isn't there a Code Purple? Or Orange? Or Turquoise? Why are some colors considered more urgent than other colors?

Collins went around to the other side of the car and slipped into the right front seat. He put on a radio headset and grabbed a small microphone. He listened to something for a few seconds, said a few words, and then put everything back and joined C. and me.

"It's too late, Governor," he said. "There has been contact. Sorry."

" 'Sorry'? 'Contact'? What do you mean?" I turned on C. "You promised me he would be safe until we talked!"

He shrugged his shoulders.

"Art Pennington is dead!" I screamed it all the way to Adabel. "You two are murderers!"

Collins and C. said nothing. Neither moved an eye, a brow, a hair, a lip.

"You bastards! You dirty rotten killer bastards!"

I wanted to grab Collins by his perfectly combed hair and pound him into that tarmac like he was a piece of roast beef. I wanted to grab C. by his good right ear and twirl him around and around and then set him sailing into the air toward Tulsa.

I wanted to cry. I wanted to throw up. I wanted out of there. I wanted to go home.

I wanted to be somebody else.

I ran right to the Beechcraft as fast as I have ever run. I yelled at the pilot to take me back to Oklahoma City as fast as he could fly.

From the airport, at my request, Springer and Autry drove me home Code Red. As fast as the Chrysler Imperial would go.

Jackie had just arrived home and gotten off the phone.

She was in the kitchen and in a frenzied, angry, crying state.

"Oh, Mack, thank God you're here. Somebody shot our store operator in Utoka. It was a robbery. Shot him with a machine gun. He's still alive. They've taken him to Dallas for special surgery.

"All the robber took was two Heath bars and a Pepsi, Mack. That's all the robber took. Two Heath bars and a Pepsi. What is this world turning into? Oh my God, Mack. What an awful, awful thing. What is happening?"

I held her hard against me as we both cried and cried.

I went about my business the next morning as acting governor of Oklahoma. I smiled while five ladies from Bartlesville presented me with a pink rose to signify the opening of the 14th Annual Northeastern Oklahoma Rose and Casserole Festival. While four fire chiefs gave me my honorary membership card from the Oklahoma Fire Chiefs' Association, which was holding its annual convention at the Park Plaza downtown. While two social-work leaders pleaded with me to oppose Buffalo Joe's proposal to release the "mildly ill" from the state's mental hospital in Ponca City. While two state senators urged me to support the plan because of overcrowding and money problems. While my secretary told me about her and her sister's tearful decision to put their eighty-four-year-old mother in a Cordell nursing home. While declining on the phone an Enid oilman's invitation to address the men's Sunday-school class at his Baptist church. While signing the routine authorization needed to pay the state workers of Oklahoma. While agreeing on the phone with the mayor of Duncan to address the annual Chamber of Commerce dinner next month. While listening to the state's three largest Chevrolet dealers complain about the unfairness of our bidding system that again awarded the contract for new highway department pickup trucks to Ford.

Jackie called just before noon.

"He's dead, Mack," she said. "Our Utoka man is dead. His friend Mr. Hagood just called from Utoka. He said he had met you. Find the killer, Mack. Tell your friend C. to find the deranged madman who did this. A message must be sent to the people of Oklahoma that deranged madmen cannot just walk into a JackieMart and murder the manager with a machine gun. Do not let Oklahoma become a jungle, Mack. It is time for drastic action. You are the governor. Order your friend C. and the highway patrol and everyone else with a gun and a nose to find the person who did this so he can be tried and electrocuted."

"Yes, ma'am," I said.

"Tommy Walt was just by here. He's looking for some advice on expansion. I was too upset to talk to him. Will you?"

"You're the businessman in the family, not me."

Janice Alice gave me the hi sign from the door. It was time for me to go. I had to address a luncheon session of the annual convention of the Oklahoma Cattlemen's Association at the Sheraton.

"The serious business is to think of a name," I said to Jackie before hanging up. "He must call it something besides T.W. Grease Collectors."

"How about something religious? Or how about McDonald's? Right, that's it. Call it McDonald's."

On another day, in another world, I might have laughed at the sparkling wit of my wife, the wonder-woman founder and owner of JackieMarts.

I told the cattlemen that I thought cows were as important to our Sooner State as oil and gas. I told them our administration was committed to putting a piece of beef on every plate at every meal of every Sooner citizen every Oklahoma day of the year. I said that how go cattle and beef, so goes Oklahoma. I said the real governor had personally asked me to personally say to them, "Cows are as sacred in Oklahoma as they are in India. On an Oklahoma road, even the governor and the lieutenant governor and the entire state government would move to one side and pass reverently on by."

There was wild applause when I finished. If Hastings Sanders had been in the audience, I'm sure he would have stood and yelled "Lie!" And I might have joined him.

I returned to my office to find on my desk the proclamation establishing Put Oklahoma Towns on the Globe Week in Oklahoma. Janice Alice had had somebody in the secretary of state's office draft it and then reproduce it on fancy heavy white paper. It was like a high school diploma, only larger and more elaborate, and said:

Whereas, it has been determined that few Oklahoma cities and towns are printed on the geographical globes sold and used throughout the world,

Whereas, this globe gap is a detriment to Oklahoma's being accorded its proper place in the world consciousness,

175

Whereas, it is deemed beneficial to the economic and spiritual well-being of the people of the State of Oklahoma that this consciousness be raised,

It is hereby proclaimed that the Week of June 17 through June 23, in the year of our Lord Nineteen Hundred and Seventy-four, be designated Put Oklahoma Towns on the Globe Week.

It gave me a reason to talk to Bill Hagood. I placed the call myself to the First Utoka National Bank.

"I'm so sorry about Art," I said immediately.

"Thank you, Governor. Thank you. It's been a terrible shock for all of us. Particularly those of us in Rotary who knew him. We read and hear about violent crime happening all of the time other places, but until it happens right here on your own doorstep to somebody you know ... well, it's just not real, I guess."

"When's the funeral? I'd like to come."

"There won't be one. The family asked that his body be cremated and the ashes sent back to Hungary."

Cremated and sent back to Hungary?

"Do the Utoka police have any clues about who did it?"

"No, sir. I was just down there. All they know is that the motive was robbery. One man. Wearing a mask. The other employees there at the JackieMart haven't been able to add very much else."

One man. Wearing a mask.

"Did the robber say anything before he shot Art?"

There was a slight hesitation before Bill Hagood said, "I think so. You might want to check all of this with your Mr. Hayes of the OBI. He's seems to be very much on top of the situation."

Yes, sir.

Then I told him about the proclamation.

"We can make a big deal out of this if you wish. Have a public ceremony in the big reception room they call the Blue Room. I'd love for you to come to Oklahoma City for it. We can get the boys and girls from the capitol press corps to maybe do a story if you want."

"I think I'll pass on that, Governor. It's a busy time here at the bank and around town. But thank you for asking me. And thank you so much for doing the proclaiming. You are doing good things for Oklahoma."

Oh, yes sir. Good things for Oklahoma was what I was doing.

Like letting agents of the United States of America and the State of Oklahoma get away with letting a young Russian KGB assassin get away with murder.

I wanted to call Brother Walt. I wanted him to know I had failed. I wanted him to fall to his knees in front of another park bench and ask His forgiveness for my not being smart enough and tough enough to prevent the murder of the Sooner Spy. He hated flying in small planes but he had offered to go to Utoka with me. I should have taken him up on it. Maybe then I would never have let Pennington out of my sight there at the airport.

I wanted him to tell me what to do now.

No.

I had Janice Alice tell Springer and Autry to bring the car around to the west basement entrance. I needed to get out and away. I needed to think about what kind of person I really was. I needed to make some decisions. On my own.

All alone.

I told Springer just to start driving.

"What direction, Governor?"

"South by southwest."

"Final destination?"

"None."

"We are required to report your final destinations to our dispatcher, sir," said Autry.

"I just changed your requirements."

"Yes sir, Governor."

I suddenly knew exactly where I was going.

"Take me to the bus museum," I told Springer.

Springer and Autry exchanged puzzled looks. "Bus museum, Governor?" Springer said.

Their ignorance was most annoying. And most indicative of the problem facing poor Fred Leon Rayburn. Fred was a driver for Oklahoma Blue Arrow Motorcoaches who'd retired at age fifty-six because he'd come into a huge amount of money. Fred had driven the same Blue Arrow schedule between Oklahoma City and Ponca City via Edmond, Guthrie, Stillwater, and Nita Pickens's hometown of Perkins Corner for twenty-two years. Five days a week every week every year for those twenty-two years, except on those rare occasions when he was sick or on vacation, he left Oklahoma City at 8:10 in the morning and arrived in Ponca City at 11:10. He departed Ponca City on the way back at 1:30, arriving in Oklahoma City at 4:30. One of his daily passengers for the last eighteen of those twenty-two years was a strange woman named Drumright: Allison Edna Patton Drumright. She got on in Guthrie and went to Stillwater, where she spent her time at the Oklahoma State University library until it was time to catch Fred's bus back in the afternoon. Nobody knew or really cared what she did at the library. Except Fred. He asked her and she said she was researching a book about the life of prehistoric women in north central Oklahoma. Every afternoon when she got back on the bus, she reported what she had found out that day. Which was never very much. But it made the time pass and Fred enjoyed the old woman's company very much. Then for five straight days she did not show up for the morning northbound bus. The first two mornings, Fred even delayed his schedule fifteen minutes waiting for her. Finally, the Guthrie bus depot manager reported the sad news that Allison Edna Patton Drumright had unexpectedly passed away, of natural causes. A few months later a lawyer in a dark suit, white shirt and black tie met the bus one morning in Oklahoma City. After establishing the fact that he was indeed Fred Leon Rayburn, the driver of the bus to Stillwater, the lawyer announced to Fred that Allison Edna Patton Drumright had left him two million dollars in her will. Fred, who was a bachelor, resigned from Oklahoma Blue Arrow that evening when he got back to Oklahoma City. It wasn't long before he was on an airplane on his first trip to Europe. He returned a month later and bought a huge house in Nichols Hills, our fanciest neighborhood, and promptly got bored and nostalgic for buses. So he decided to start a bus museum. By coincidence, Oklahoma Blue Arrow had just bought out Sooner West Coaches, a small company that ran from Oklahoma City southwest to Anadarko and north to Kingfisher and Enid. Fred bought the old Sooner West garage, put up a flashing red, white and green neon sign in front that said "National Motor

Coach Museum," and started collecting bus memorabilia to put in it.

The problem from the beginning was that few people were interested in coming to see it. It seems there was interest in museums for trains and cars but not for buses. Bus people, from the presidents of Greyhound and Trailways on down to the lowliest bus washers, came, of course, when they came through Oklahoma City. But the ordinary-public kind of people mostly did not. The Chamber of Commerce put it on the maps and in the guides of interesting places to visit, along with all the other established museums. There were museums for softball, firefighting and several other things in Oklahoma City, in addition to the big ones for the cowboys and the 45th Infantry Division. I also got the Oklahoma Tourism and Recreation Department to give the bus museum a nice write-up in its pamphlets. But nothing worked. And now, five years after it had opened its doors, it was only barely there. Fred had pretty much given up acquiring any new items of memorabilia.

So while it was annoying, it was also understandable that Springer and Autry had never heard of the museum. I gave them the address, which was off Reno Avenue west of downtown. I was pleased to hear Autry tell his dispatcher we were headed for the National Motor Coach Museum. I was sure it was the first time those words had been spoken over the Oklahoma Highway Patrol radio communications system.

It was open. I was greeted by my favorite among Fred's volunteer helpers, a little old man in an old beige American Buslines uniform, complete with cap and badge, dark red tie and ticket punch in a tan leather holster on his right hip. His name was Evans. He was my favorite because he left me alone.

Stepping inside the museum was like stepping inside a 1930s bus depot. There were a couple of Art Deco–style ticket counters and black-leather-and-chrome waiting-room chairs. The walls were covered with pictures of buses and bus depots, route maps, assemblages of tickets, timetables and bus depot signs, like the little hot Thunderbird Motor Coaches one over the storeroom in my garage. Fred did not have a Thunderbird in the collection. But he did have another of my favorites, the Texas Red Rocket Motor Bus Company, as well as signs from Bowen Motor Coaches, Santa Fe Trailways, Hudson Transit Lines, Pickwick Stages, Southern Kansas Greyhound Lines, Missouri Pacific Transportation Company, Edwards Lakes to the Sea Stages, and many from other distinguished old bus companies. I knew about some of them from the short time I had worked as a ticket agent for Thunderbird in Adabel, and the rest from reading back copies of the monthly *Russell's Official National Motor Coach Guide*s Fred had collected and stacked neatly on a table in a corner. There were several display cases of antique toy buses, including some beautiful and valuable cast-irons. There were ticket validators and punches, ashtrays with bus company emblems in the center, an array of bus steering wheels and dashboards, a display under glass of several hundred different cap badges. One wall was covered like wallpaper with rolled-out black-and-white destination signs. My favorite was from an old Thunderbird bus that was used on routes in my home Kansas country. Wichita, Marion, Emporia, Lehigh,

McPherson, Eureka, Chanute, Iola, Independence, Coffey-
ville, Parsons, Pittsburg, Topeka, Council Grove, Hering-
ton, Abilene, Junction City, Manhattan and Salina were all
on it.

I had seen all the displays several times before. I looked
around briefly again and then sat down in one of the Art
Deco chairs. Springer and Autry had stayed in the car. Evans
remained off in the corner looking at the *Russell's Guides*.
No other visitors were there.

I was letting them get away with it. I was letting my
friend, the head of the Oklahoma Bureau of Investigation,
and his friend, Collins of the CIA, get away with working
some devious Washington-ordered scheme that involved the
sacrifice of a human being's life. Sure, the guy had been a
Russian spy. But he had come over to our side and was
living a respectable American Oklahoman life as the franchisee of a JackieMart drive-thru grocery store and president
of a Rotary Club. I had failed to stop the whole thing in
the first place. Brother Walt had said to risk it. Stare them
down. The chances of the other guy's blinking are always
better if you know you never will. And C. did blink. I was
on the way. If I had only been more careful there at the
airport and held the Sooner Spy with me while I resolved
it all. Okay. What happens if I go public now? Hold a
news conference. Reveal that Art Pennington, the man
killed in the Utoka robbery, was in fact a Russian defector
who was killed by a Russian hit man. Admit that I was
an unsuspecting dupe of the assassin. Charge the CIA
and the OBI with being accomplices because they knew it
was happening and did nothing to stop it. Why did they
not stop it? Demand an answer. Confess that I stole a

Thunderbird bus depot sign from an insurance office in
Utoka. Justify it on grounds of national historical preser-
vation. Announce that I plan to call Governor Hayman in
Japan and inform him of my intention of resigning my
position as lieutenant governor of Oklahoma. Say that I
plan to go directly from the news conference to the proper
authorities for prosecution on charges of burglary. Declare
my intention of returning the Thunderbird sign to its right-
ful owner . . .

I became aware of somebody standing next to me. I looked
around and saw a pair of gray suit pants. It was C.

"I didn't know you were interested in the history of the
American motor coach," I said without looking all the way
up at his face.

"It's a secret passion of mine. The smell of diesel smoke
and dirty restroom urinals really turns me on."

"I'm thinking. Please leave me alone."

"I understand you want to know if the killer said anything
to Art Pennington before he shot him?"

They're tapping my phone! They have a bug on the
telephone of the acting governor of Oklahoma!

"Get out of here, C."

"I have come with an invitation, Mack. Colley and I would
like to show you a movie."

"Forget it."

"A movie taken in Utoka yesterday evening. It's a spy
story."

I made a decision.

I stood and summoned to my good eye the toughest, most
official, most piercing look I could.

"Under the powers vested in me as governor of Oklahoma, I hereby relieve you, C. Harry Hayes, of your duties as director of the Oklahoma Bureau of Investigation. I plan to immediately go to a justice of the peace and swear out a warrant for the arrest of you and Collins on charges of accessory to commit murder and stealing two Heath bars and a Pepsi. Please put your badge, your weapon and the keys to your office on that counter over there."

C. took two steps to a ticket counter with a cracked glass blue-and-white sign over it that said "Burlington Trailways—Bus Tickets Sold Here to the Next Town or Across America." His face was gray and fixed like a courthouse statue's. He opened his suit coat and removed his big gold badge from where it was pinned on the left side. He dropped it on the counter. He withdrew his .38 revolver from the holster on his right hip and set it gently on the counter. Then he took a key ring out of his pocket and removed four keys from it and placed them on the counter.

"Now will you come and see the movie, Mack?"

"It is hard to think how I could have been as wrong about somebody as I have been about you," I said. "And don't say anything about that Thunderbird sign. I know, I am awful, too. I will resign and take my punishment...."

"Okay, Mack, fine. But please come with me to my office first."

"It's not your office anymore. I just fired you."

"Okay. Come with me anywhere you wish. But let Colley and me talk to you. He is violating every rule in his book, but I have convinced him he must tell you the whole story. Please, Mack. Please. There is always time for you to do all of the rest. Resign, hang yourself and me. Whatever."

It made sense. So I made another decision.

"All right. Pick up your keys and put your badge and gun back on," I said. "You are herby unfired. For a while."

·13·

Sooner Sweets
and Nuts

C. TOOK ME to a gray room at OBI headquarters, behind a gray door. Collins was there. So were half a dozen or so gray leather chairs, a movie projector on a table, and a small white movie screen pulled down out of the ceiling near the far wall.

Collins said nothing to me. I had nothing to say to him.

C. turned on the projector.

The movie was in black and white. There was Calvin getting into a Chevrolet van. He was dressed in uniform work clothes. "Sooner Sweets and Nuts" was painted on the side of the van.

There was sound. I could hear the motor being revved up. And there were other vehicle noises. It was on a busy street in Utoka.

The picture cut to a shot of the van driving down Main

Street, then left on Wilson and right on Seminole to the JackieMart. It pulled up to the rear, near the door marked "Employees and Deliveries Only."

Calvin stepped out of the van and went to the door. There was a dark ski-mask thing over his face. He was carrying a long thin cardboard box. He pushed a doorbell.

The picture cut to a view from inside the JackieMart. I heard the buzz of the doorbell. A young woman went to the door. She pushed a button that activated a two-way radio communication system.

"Hi," she said. "May I help you?"

"Hi, I'm from Sooner Sweets and Nuts," said Calvin. "I have a special delivery here for Mr. Pennington. It's sweets. Candy and nuts and things."

"Sure," said the woman. "Hold on."

She went to the other side of the large room, where her fellow workers were racing around to fill orders from customers driving through on the other side. I heard her say, "Mr. Pennington, there's somebody at the back door with something special and sweet for you."

Then Art Pennington, the Sooner Spy, came into view. He walked to the door. He reached for the doorknob. He turned it. The door opened. Calvin was pointing the long thin box right at Art.

Calvin said: "This is a holdup. I want two Heath bars and a Pepsi."

Art hollered at his employees to remain still and silent. Then he asked one to bring him two Heath bars and a Pepsi.

She did, and dashed away out of harm's way. Art handed the items to Calvin.

187

Calvin said: "Thank you, Traitor Aleksander Andreavich Pronnikov."

There was the sound and sight of a machine gun. I had never seen or heard a real one in action before. *Pop-pop-pop. Pop-pop-pop.* It sounded like a child breaking balloons with a pin. It looked like little flash bulbs going off.

Art fell backward to the floor.

The picture cut back to the outside. Calvin jumped into his van and burned rubber away. He took a series of turns and finally stopped behind a clump of trees, where a four-door Dodge sedan was parked. He removed his mask and uniform, and put his right leg into the leg of a pair of suit trousers.

And then from the trees came dozens of men carrying pistols and rifles. Calvin was surrounded and subdued, frisked and handcuffed before he even had a chance to react.

Next Calvin was sitting in what looked like a hotel or motel room.

"We know who you are," said a voice. It was Collins's voice. The picture stayed on Calvin. "We have on film your every movement since you arrived in Utoka. The film includes you arriving at the JackieMart and committing murder. Would you like to see the film?"

"No," said Calvin. He clearly had not lost his composure. They had also clearly let him finish dressing before bringing him to wherever he was. He was in full suit and tie and looked neat and tidy and smart and eager. Almost exactly the way he did when he went through the receiving line after Oklahoma Southeastern commencement.

My God, how long ago and in what other world had that been?

The room in the film went dark. And on a small screen came that climactic scene: Calvin, in his mask, emerging from the van, the woman inside summoning the Sooner Spy, the getting and the delivering of the Heath bars and the Pepsi, Calvin saying, "Thank you, Traitor Aleksander Andreavich Pronnikov," and then the *pop-pop-pop* and flashes of machine-gun fire.

The lights came back on in the room. "The question now," said another man's voice, "is, what we do with the film? The answer is yours. The decision is yours."

"I have nothing to say to you now or at any other time about anything," Calvin said. He was still smooth and smart.

Collins said: "Let me lay out the options for you. The first would be simply to hand you and the film over to the Oklahoma authorities. With the evidence provided by this film I would expect a jury of Oklahomans would take about ten seconds to find you guilty of murder. Oklahoma, as you probably know from your KGB briefings, is a death-penalty state. That means you would soon after be seated in an electric chair, where you would remain until your insides are thoroughly toasted and you are dead. I would imagine the publicity surrounding this would be spectacular."

Another male voice said: "There could be a public outcry of unprecedented proportions. I would imagine that our president and our Congress and our news media and our public would be outraged to learn beyond even a shadow of a doubt that the government of the Soviet Union had sanctioned an assassination on our shores. I could see the film being played over and over again on our television networks. I could see it also being shown to a hushed special session of the United Nations General Assembly. Can you see all of this happening too ... Mr. .... what should we call you? What is your real name?"

Calvin said nothing.

Collins spoke again: "Very well. Let's look at another option. There is no publicity. There is no arrest, no involvement of Oklahoma or any other authorities. We merely make a copy of the film and deliver it in an unmarked, untraceable envelope to the Soviet ambassador in Washington. My, what a surprise and disappointment it would be for him and his colleagues in Moscow to discover that their adversaries have film of a Russian operative committing murder on U.S. soil. We would, of course, release you from our custody. You would be free to go and to return to duty. We might even consider depositing you at the Russian embassy in Washington along with the film. At any rate, you are clearly a clever and resourceful young man, and I am sure you can convince your superiors that you can still be a valuable member of your country's intelligence service. If that's not practical, I would hope that they would at least give you some kind of hearing or trial before taking disciplinary action. What is the going punishment now for Soviet agents who cause international incidents that are severely and monumentally detrimental to the image and function of their government?"

Calvin had no answer.

Collins continued: "Very well. Let's look at one other option that is a bit more relaxed. We send no film to anyone. Not to authorities here, not to your people. We make no copies. We merely put that film into a very secure safe place and forget it. You get up from that chair and walk out of that door a free man. As far as anyone knows, the killing of Art Pennington was just what you wanted it to look like. A random killing by a madman capitalist pig American thug with a thing for Heath bars and Pepsi. You join your KGB colleague where he's waiting for you in Oklahoma City— Levikov is his name, I believe—and you go on and follow the safe escape route as planned, to return to your superiors a hero. Bravo! You carried out an official death sentence on a traitor to Mother Russia. Bravo! There would be decorations and promotions. You would be earmarked for a fast-track career to the very top of the KGB. Soon you would be a station chief, then an assistant deputy head of a directorate. Who knows where and how far you could go up that ladder to success?"

Calvin was listening. He was almost smiling. I had already figured out what was coming next. Clearly, he had too. So he finished it himself.

"And all I have to do is betray my country for the rest of my life, of course. If I refuse, you send off the film. If I ever want to stop betraying my country, you send off the film. If you ever decide I am doubling back by giving you bad information, you send off the film. Always, you can send off the film. One way I am ruined and dead, the other way I am a traitor to my country."

Nobody said anything for at least half a minute.

Then Collins said: "As we said at the beginning of our time together, the decision is yours."

C. leaned across the table and turned off the projector.

And the overhead lights came on.

Collins was in the chair on my left. "If anyone in my agency ever finds out that I showed you this film, it is lights

191

out for me, Governor. You now have me by the same parts of my anatomy that we had your young Russian friend."

I turned to C. in the chair on my right. "Then that makes us all even-steven."

"Not quite," Collins said. "Not quite even or steven. You have the ability to blow this entire operation. One public word from you and it is all over. And I don't mean for us personally. I mean for this operation.

"Now at least I hope you understand, Governor. Washington wanted to see if the young one could be turned. That would be quite a coup, as I am sure you realize. To have a young up-and-coming source inside the KGB was worth the risk, in their opinion. . . ."

"The risk of a man's life," I said. "It was worth it, all right. Worth it to everybody but him."

"He was an intelligence officer. He chose that life just like I did. It's dangerous. It's a life of day-to-day expendability. In my and Pronnikov's line of work you can't take death personally. He would have been the first to understand what we did, and applaud us for it."

"Don't call him Pronnikov. He was Art Pennington, a prominent citizen of Utoka, Oklahoma. He loved his new life. You let a Russian assassin murder Art Pennington, president of the Utoka Rotary Club and the owner of a JackieMart–Utoka. Calling him Pronnikov is not going to change that."

"Governor, there is a war going on. Bullets are not being fired all the time but it is real. It's a battle between the good guys and the bad guys. . . ."

"Good guys do not use their fellow human beings as tadpoles on the end of fishing lines."

"I am sorry you feel that way."

"I am ashamed for you that you do not."

C. finally spoke: "Mack, I don't like this any better than you. But this spying is another league, another world from what we are used to here in Oklahoma. It'll make sense sometime. Sometime it'll make sense...."

"You make me sick, C."

I stood to go.

"Are you going to tell me the ending of the movie?" I said. "What option did Calvin choose?"

Collins said: "I cannot say. I only told you as much as I did because ... well, C. said it might be helpful."

"Because I blackmailed you. The acting governor of Oklahoma blackmailed the director of the OBI and an agent of the CIA into telling him why they allowed a Sooner citizen to be murdered."

C. said: "I know it doesn't matter, but you should know, Mack, that Colley hasn't even told me everything either. I don't know what the KGB kid chose to do. All I know is what you know. I haven't seen any more of the film than you. It's all need-to-know."

I wanted to scream. But I didn't. I wanted to throw something at somebody. But I didn't. I just left the room and headed for Springer and Autry and the black Imperial.

C. followed me to the entrance. "Mack, is it over? Do you plan to take any action of any kind? We have to know...."

"It's over. We all have too much on each other. I'm not going to do anything. Case closed. I won't blow the operation. It's over. The Sooner Spy's dead."

I stepped outside into the Oklahoma sunshine.

"Mack, someday you will find it in your heart to understand and to forgive me. I value your friendship and respect more than any other living human's. With time and distance it'll be all right. It must be. You're my sanity, Mack."

"But I'm also a burglar, C."

I shook his hand. He really was a fine man.

Fine as I was, at least.

·14·
The End?

THE STORY was not over yet. At least I don't *think* it was. I am convinced there were a couple more twists and turns. I can't prove anything, but I know what I believe.

There was something about it all that smelled wrong from the beginning. The beginning after that end. Not the moral wrong that had already upset me so. But the *wrong* wrong. Fact wrong.

When I was seven years old in Kansas, an uncle who drove a butane gas truck told me he could smell a lie. He said it was as easy as walking up the aisle of a crowded bus and picking out the dill-pickle eaters from the fried-onion eaters.

I had driven away sniffing from the gray OBI building that afternoon.

C. and Collins, two upright government servants, had just

confirmed to me in deepest, darkest confidence that for the good of America, the Sooner Spy, Utoka's JackieMart franchisee and Rotary Club president, had been shot to death while the CIA, the FBI and the OBI watched and took pictures. It was the right thing to do because it forced a rotten Communist KGB killer who looked like a Choctaw to turn traitor. I had just seen the film, hadn't I? And why would anybody make up a lie about such an awful story of human sacrifice? So what was the problem?

So my nose was full of fried onion. That was the problem.

But I decided right there and then that there was nothing I could do about it. Or should. Nothing. I wanted the whole Sooner Spy thing out of my head. I wanted to get back to enjoying being the acting governor. And a regular person. And father. I was even willing to want to get back to worrying about Tommy Walt's restaurant grease collection business.

So whatever my doubts, whatever the onion smells, the terrible case of the Sooner Spy was closed. Over and done. Just as I had promised C.

In a few days, it was back to being the Second Man of Oklahoma. Buffalo Joe returned. And he returned with a new dumb idea.

"Japan, Mack. Japan. That is the place that has the solution to all of our problems. That's because we have the solution to all of their problems. Get it, Mack? They have a problem we can solve, we have a problem they can solve. They have money. Lots and lots of money. You can smell it, Mack. I promise you, you can smell it. Dollars and their things called yen smell the same. It's everywhere. The smell of money. But they also have a serious land shortage. Maybe the most serious land shortage in the world. All they have is a bunch of tiny islands. A square inch of land in downtown Tokyo is worth ten thousand dollars. That's right, Mack. They're selling land in downtown Tokyo for ten thousand dollars a square inch. All they have are a bunch of tiny islands with too many people who have too much money. So what does that make you think of? What does it make you think of? Look out of that window over there, Mack. Just look out of this window over there."

We were at lunch the day of his return. Just the two of us, so I could brief him on what had happened in the Sooner State during his absence. We were at the Petroleum Club, which was on the twenty-fourth floor of the Oklahoma Bank and Trust Building, the tallest building in Oklahoma City. We were at an isolated table for two.

I looked out of that window over there. It was a blue crystal day. The kind that could inspire the right person to write a musical about Oklahoma if it hadn't already been done.

"What do you see, Mack? Tell me what you see."

What I saw was the tops of smaller office buildings and then the courthouse and city hall and the airport off to the southwest and cars and streets and highways and trucks and people who looked like bugs.

"You see land, Mack. That is what you see. You see land. What do we have more of in Oklahoma than any other thing? You know what the answer is? Land is what we have. We have land. Get it, Mack? We have an abundance of what they have a shortage of. They need land, we have land. They have money, we need money. So what do we do, Mack? What do we do?"

"Sell Oklahoma to Japan? Come on, Joe. If we sold Oklahoma to Japan it wouldn't be Oklahoma anymore. Besides, there is a language problem...."

"Not all of Oklahoma. Not the whole thing. Just the parts we don't need. The parts that are just lying out there."

"What parts, Joe?"

"The vacant parts. The parts nobody's using. The dry land out in the Panhandle, some of that wood and forest stuff down north of Hugotown. Some in the cities. The parts nobody's using and nobody ever will use."

"What will Japan use it for?"

"For plants and factories and offices and farms and things. The same kinds of things Americans use it for. The exact same things we use it for."

A couple of years before, Joe had had another idea. It was finally to put a dome on our state capitol, the only capitol building in the nation that did not have a dome. That was because the money had run out in 1915 when it was being built and no governor or legislature since had decided it was important enough to do anything about Oklahoma's dome-less condition. Nothing came of Joe's campaign after a dome expert from Cincinnati studied the situation and said it would cost $15 million to put a first-class one up there. So after a few months Joe and the rest of Oklahoma forgot it. But while it was hot he went around saying it was time to crown Oklahoma. And "Crown Oklahoma" became his password greeting and good-bye phrase to everybody. I wondered now if "Sell Oklahoma" would be the one for this idea.

But I did not ask him. He did not say, "Sell Oklahoma, Mack." And I did not reply, "Sell Oklahoma, Joe." I just said, "You are a man of ideas, Joe. A man of ideas."

"Thank you, Mack. I will need your help on this. I will need your help. Some of our Neanderthals are not going to go for selling off our Sooner land to the little yellow Japs. I can hear them talking now about Pearl Harbor and Brian Donlevy at Wake Island, John Wayne at Iwo. Some of our Neanderthals are not going to like it one bit. But it'll save us, Mack. It'll pick up our economy and keep it picked up. We have the land. Why not use it for the good of Oklahoma? We have the land. Why not let an old enemy make amends? Look at it as war reparations. Right. War reparations. How about that? Forgive and forget, and here's a really swell five blocks of downtown Muskogee that's for sale."

"What about Texas?"

"Texas?"

"They have a lot more useless land to sell than we do. What if they set up shop in competition?"

"They're not smart enough. They are just not smart enough, Mack."

I asked about the governors' conference. He dismissed it with a wave and an attack on Los Angeles.

"Stay away from Los Angeles, Mack. Stay *way* away. Years of inhaling smog and avoiding death on freeways have made them different. The people, I mean. The people of Los Angeles. They're all the color of chili pepper. All of them. Even the blacks tan themselves. Even the blacks. Everybody uses too much soap and water and deodorant. On themselves and their cars. Stay away from Los Angeles, Mack. I had the Los Angeles nightmare again on the way home on the plane. I swear I did. I swear. I dozed off while reading one of the governors' conference reports on welfare reform. It was about a plan to just give every poor person cash. Forget public housing and food stamps and all the rest.

Just send them a check every month and fire all social workers and everybody else involved except the guy who makes
out the checks. Give every poor person cash. Forget the rest.
I woke up screaming. I dreamed I was the governor of Los
Angeles instead of Oklahoma."

It was only as he was signing a prominent oilman's name
to our lunch check that he asked about my eleven days as
acting governor.

"How did it go? Anything happen I need to know about?"

"Not a thing. Everything was strictly routine. Strictly
routine."

And the case of the Sooner Spy would have probably
stayed out of my mind and everything would have really
been routine if I were not a man who kept his promises to
God. Brother Walt had forced me to promise out loud to
God to return the Thunderbird sign. It was a side deal he
forced on me as part of the plan we hatched to save the
Sooner Spy's life. The one I botched by letting Art leave the
Utoka airport.

"That sign is like a spot of devil acid on a clean white
shirt, Mack. It will burn a hole in your skin, in your heart,
in your soul, in your life forever," Brother Walt had said.
"Rid yourself of it. Return it. Purge it."

I argued that the stupid and evil attitude of the Utoka
Sparrow toward the history of the motor coach made my
continued possession of the sign permissible, probably even
to God. It was a thin argument, and I dropped it cold when
he reminded me of the peril.

He said:

"All right, Mack. Keep the sign. Keep the knowledge

that it is hidden under some blankets in your garage. Keep it in your mind when you shave in the morning. When you drive to work. When the phone rings. When you drive through a McDonald's or a Burger King. Or a JackieMart. When you enter a church of the Holy Road. When you watch the news or whatever on the television. When you live and breathe every second from this day forward. Is this it? Is this the call? Will this be the day? Will this be the day somebody comes knocking on my life's door? Hello there, Mr. Lieutenant Governor of Oklahoma, I have a friend who murdered his cousin I would like released from prison, and if you don't do it I will send you there to replace him for having committed burglary in Utoka. Hello there, Mack. You remember me? I met you one time on a tour of our beloved state capitol building. Well, I need a state road paved. It runs in front of my barbecue carry-out in Vinita. Pave it, Mack, or I will tell the world about that Thunderbird sign in your garage. . . . "

"Nobody in Vinita or anywhere else is going to find out about it," I said. Ignorantly.

"Well, now let's look at that. *I* know about it. Your friend C. knows about it. His friend from the CIA knows about it. Well, now aren't you the one who said to me that there is no such thing as a secret? All it takes is one of three of us to tell another in strictest confidence. . . . "

"What if I presented it as an anonymous gift to the National Motor Coach Museum? I know the guy who runs it. He does not have a Thunderbird in the collection."

Brother Walt shook his head, and on the sixth day after Buffalo Joe returned to Oklahoma and I returned to being lieutenant governor, I gave it back. I gave it back the way I got it. The Risk It way.

I could have taken the easy way out. I could have just put the sign between two pieces of cardboard and mailed it to the Utoka Sparrow. Anonymously, of course. Or sent it to him as package express on the bus. Collect, of course. Oklahoma Blue Arrow Motorcoaches ran five round trips a day from Oklahoma City to Utoka.

Instead.

I drove that day to Wilburton for an early-evening dedication of a small outdoor recreation and picnic area named in honor of Bud Wilkinson, the best and most famous football coach in the history of the University of Oklahoma.

Utoka was on the road between Wilburton and Oklahoma City. It was dark when I came back through. My Buick's headlights caught the Rotary sign. The one that said "Meets Thursday, 12 noon, Best Western–Utoka Inn." I drove directly to the Utoka Sparrow's insurance office. I tried not to look at the JackieMart next door. But I couldn't help it. It was open for business. A wreath was on the door.

I parked again right in front of the insurance office. I got out and went around to the trunk and removed the Thunderbird sign, which was still wrapped inside the old blankets from my garage.

I walked around to the rear door of the office so I would be out of sight of anyone who might have driven or walked by. Just as before.

From a coat pocket I removed a pair of leather gloves and put them on. Then I took out a coping-saw blade and a screwdriver from the same pocket.

The door opened easily. Just as before. Quickly, stealthily,

I again found the closet. I opened it. I removed the sign from the blankets, which I then used to wipe the sign clean. As any smart burglar would do.

I placed that gorgeous thing back on the closet floor where I had found it. And left the building.

Just as before.

As I drove away again, also as before, I thought about what I would have said if I had been caught:

Well, you see, it was like this, Officer. There I was, driving along the road from Wilburton, and what do I see in a ditch off to the right? An old Thunderbird bus depot sign that I knew just had to belong to a young insurance man in Utoka. So I decided to return it. It was late and I didn't want to disturb anyone so I let myself into the office and put it in the first closet I came to. Call it a burglary in reverse. Instead of committing burglary to take something, I committed a burglary to put something back. Call it a Robin Hood kind of thing.

Did you say "Robin Hood," Mr. Lieutenant Governor?

Yes, Officer. Robin Hood was a young man like you who believed that . . .

Please be informed, sir, that you have the constitutional right to remain silent. But if you do choose to make a statement anything you say may be used against you in a court of law. You have a right to legal counsel. Now, if you will please hold your hands out in front of you, I will place the cuffs on your wrists.

There was a traffic light one block past the insurance office on the way out of town toward Oklahoma City. It was red. I stopped. My eye wandered to a large hand-lettered poster on a pole off to the right.

<small>TONIGHT</small>!
At the Utoka High Auditorium!
The Community Singers present *Oklahoma!*
Come hear Will Johnson the crooning coach,
Bill Hagood the singing banker, Allison
Dean Mays the warbling nurse . . .

Bill Hagood the singing banker.
Bill Hagood the singing banker?
The light turned green and I drove into a Derby Oil station on the next corner and asked for directions to Utoka High.
The performance was about to begin. It was sold out. But at the door a young woman with the look of a high school biology teacher said it would be fine for me to stand in the back.
I had seen *Oklahoma!* at least twenty times. Maybe twenty-five. I knew it cold. So I knew from the second I stepped inside the auditorium when Curly would be singing "The Surrey with the Fringe on Top."
And there he came. Played by Bill Hagood. Bill Hagood the singing banker. He opened his mouth and out came those marvelous words:

"Chicks and ducks and geese better scurry
When I take you out in the surrey,
When I take you out in the surrey with the fringe on top.
Watch that fringe and see how it flutters
When I drive them high-stepping strutters;
Nosy folks will peek through the shutters and their eyes
will pop.

The wheels are yellow, the upholstery's brown,
The dashboard's genuine leather,
With isinglass curtains you can roll down in case
there's a change in the weather...."

And the words came out in a marvelous way. Bill wasn't
Gordon MacRae but he was good. *Very* good. Better than
anybody else I had ever heard in person sing the part of
Curly.

So?

So Calvin shot the wrong man? So Bill Hagood was the
real Sooner Spy? But then who was Art Pennington? The
Utoka contact? The CIA sacrificed its own man in order to
snag a new source inside the KGB?

I had a new smell in my nostrils. It was fresh. And much
more tart and sour than fried onions.

First thing the next morning, I asked Janice Alice to check
the records of the Oklahoma Banking Commission. I wanted
copies of everything having to do with the First National
Bank of Utoka and Bill Hagood.

A few hours later, I happened to be out in the western
part of Oklahoma City. I had just spoken to the Northwest
Oklahoma City Kiwanis meeting and decided to swing by
and see my lovely and talented wife as long as I was in the
neighborhood.

She was surprised to see me, since I had not said anything
at breakfast about stopping by. The people in her office were
nicer to me than usual. Everybody always was, immediately
after I had been acting governor of Oklahoma.

She had somebody bring me a cup of coffee and we sat

down on her office couch. It was clear from the way she pursed her lips that she had more important things to do than chat with her husband. It was clear from the way she stared at me that she was trying to figure out why I was there. I had never ever just dropped by in the middle of the afternoon.

I made some very small small-talk and then expressed again my shock and sorrow about Art Pennington.

"I'm sorry to say there's still no break in the case," I said.

"There had better be soon," she said. "Our people and everybody else who works at drive-thrus and 7-Elevens and Circle Ks are scared. Two of our franchisees have said they want out."

"I was really impressed with Art Pennington," I said, getting down to business. "Are all of your franchisees of that high quality?"

"Not really," she said. She was getting ready to throw me out. "He was a cut above most, I guess."

"How did he happen to get the Utoka store anyhow? One of the investigators was asking me about that."

"I don't remember all of the details. I've got his store file around here somewhere. We got it out when it all happened down there."

She went to her desk and looked at the tabs on a stack of five or six file folders neatly arranged on the left-hand corner of her desk.

"Here it is," she said. "It's all in here. Why don't you take it?"

"Sure..."

"And Mack, unless there's something else, I am already late for a meeting with the accountants."

"I'm on my way." I leaned across, kissed her on the lips

and walked briskly for the door with that file tucked snugly under my arm.

"Mack," she said, stopping me. "Are you sure you didn't have something else on your mind? Is Tommy Walt all right? Have you heard something about the girls?"

"Everything's fine. Thanks. See you tonight."

"There's no crisis in the government of Oklahoma that I don't know about, is there?"

"No, ma'am."

I did not know exactly what I was looking for, but I was certain I would know when I found it. And I was right.

From a file of Xeroxed bank records came the information that William White Hagood came to Utoka four years before. He purchased a sizable minority interest in the bank in a cash transaction negotiated by a Chicago bank broker. The records showed the Utoka bank was in some mild financial difficulty at the time and it needed both money and new leadership.

From the JackieMart file came the information that Arthur Wilson Pennington came to Utoka two weeks after Bill Hagood. All the financing for the $174,000 used to purchase the real estate and construct the JackieMart was handled by the First National Bank of Utoka. The loan officer was listed as William Hagood.

So? So isn't it interesting that the two of them came to town at about the same time? So how come a stranger can just walk into a town from nowhere and buy into a local bank and become its president? And so how come another stranger can come into that bank from nowhere two weeks later and borrow $174,000?

While I was reading over those files I remembered something else. When C. came to the bus museum to find me that afternoon I saw the movie of the killing, he said he heard I had asked whether Calvin said anything before he shot Art. I assumed he knew about my conversation with Hagood because he was tapping my phone. But it could have been simply because Bill Hagood told Collins.

As, of course, he would if he were the real Sooner Spy.

The problem with my theory was murder. The more I thought about it, the more I realized it was both crazy and un-American. It's one thing to let one Russian kill another Russian. But set up a deal to allow a Russian to kill an American just on the possibility of then blackmailing the killer into becoming a secret turncoat? Tilt. It made no sense, even in our non-Oklahoma spy world C. had talked about. If Art Pennington, or whoever he really was, was a CIA agent or some such thing, it made even less sense. No CIA or some such agency of the United States of America would ever, *ever* let one of its own be slaughtered that way.

So? So I called Brother Walt in Adabel.

I asked if he knew any Holy Road preachers in the Dallas area who could be depended on to carry out a delicate and confidential mission. He said he did know one. A man named Owens who pastored the First Church of the Holy Road in Garland, a Dallas suburb.

"Would he be willing to lie for a greater good?" I asked.

"Depends on the lie," said Brother Walt. "Only the Heavenly Father has the ultimate power to judge what is a lie and what is not a lie. It is not for us mere mortals to make such decisions. What's the lie?"

"He would have to say he was ministering to the bereaved family of a recently deceased citizen."

There was only a slight pause before he said: "Then what?"

I pronounced the mission: Under the cover of clergy, find out all there was to know about the death of one Arthur Pennington. When did he die? Was there an autopsy? Was he cremated in Dallas or sent somewhere else? Is there a doctor or nurse or hospital worker who actually saw the body?

"I will see what I can do, Mack."

"Thanks, Walt."

"You do know, do you not, that these spy things can get pretty rough at times?" he said. "Even American spy things."

"So?"

"So you may be driving down a muddy red dead-end road. So maybe they used one of their own as bait. So maybe they handed him over like a golden collection plate. I'll be in touch."

Golden collection plate?

That's it!

Tommy Walt was sitting behind his desk in the back of the warehouse. Three other men were crowded around him. They were in coats and ties. Tommy Walt was in his official coveralls. Tommy Walt, like his mother before him, did not seem that pleased to see me. He, too, was busy. But he did introduce me to the three men. None of them seemed to know that I was the lieutenant governor of Oklahoma, and he did not tell them. He said they were owners of other restaurant grease collection companies in the Oklahoma City area. They had gathered to form a trade association to protect their shared business interests and to defend themselves from dishonest and violent competitors.

A trade association. That meant that one day I would probably find myself as lieutenant governor or even as acting governor signing a proclamation for Restaurant Grease Collection Week in Oklahoma or presenting a plaque to the Restaurant Grease Collector of the Year.

I asked Tommy Walt if I could see him privately for just a minute.

He excused himself and followed me to the drum rack.

"I have only four words to speak," I said in a heavy whisper. "Ready?"

"Sure, Dad," he replied.

"Those four words are: 'The Golden Collection Plate.'"

His facial expression did not change.

"The Golden Collection Plate," I said again.

"Dad, what are you talking about?"

"I am talking about a name for your business."

"I've gotten used to the one it has. Mom has her whole first name in her company's name. I don't see why I can't have my initials in mine if I want to."

"Think about it. The Golden Collection Plate. Imagine how classy it would look painted on the side of your truck, on the sign outside...."

"I'll think about it, Dad. I really will. Thanks. Was there something else?"

"No, that was it."

He glanced back at the three men and leaned over to me. Now it was his turn to whisper. "What I'm really planning is to buy these guys out. There are a lot of efficiencies of scale to be made. Cheaper rates on drums, better utilization of trucks and personnel. The bank's interested in financing it."

"Sounds great. Good luck, son."

"Thanks, Dad. I'll never forget how you helped me that first night."

"Glad I could do it. How is that part of it going?"

"Better. I've got one permanent employee now. An OU Ph.D. in medieval intellectual history, if you can believe that. He's waiting for a teaching job somewhere, and he writes poetry about war in the daytime, so it's perfect."

"Ask him about The Golden Collection Plate."

"He's not religious. He probably wouldn't even know what it meant."

Brother Walt was back to me in two days with the following report:

"Nobody named Art Pennington died in Dallas on the date he was supposed to have died or on any other day around that time or place. That's no big deal on the face of it, because they could have had him die under another name. The problem with that is that no hospital emegency room down there has any record of a man being flown in on a helicopter from Utoka. No funeral home did any cremating of any Utoka citizens, and they did not do any shipping of bodies back to Michigan or Hungary on the right dates either. My preacher friend checked the police, the medical examiner and all of the other people you should check for any and all information. Nothing. He also said it was easy and he didn't even have to test the temptation to lie. People don't mind telling you somebody didn't die in their town. Even in Texas.

"Now, Mack, this may not mean what you think it means. The spy people may have only said they flew him to Dallas in order to throw off the Commies. They may have actually taken him to some godless place like Hot Springs or Little Rock where he really did die. Remain calm and smart about this. Don't let your wish for something make you see something that isn't there. It's okay for preachers, but not for ordinary people like lieutenant governors.

"God is Great, Mack."

I was no expert on friendship. I had not had that many real friends, particularly after I lost my eye. Jackie's first husband, Tom Bell Pepper Bowen, was the first, and that didn't last long because he died. Brother Walt came into my life when I lived in Adabel and had been in my life ever since. I considered him a friend even though he was a preacher and was much older than I was. Who ever heard of having a preacher as a friend? But there had not been many others. Particularly after I went into politics. Buffalo Joe was right when he told me politics was a place where everybody was your friend and so nobody was. I hoped he was probably wrong when he said: "Nobody loves a politician except his grandchildren, his wife's relatives and people he appointed to office. Sad but true, Mack. True but sad."

We had a neighbor in Oklahoma City I liked. But he was a lawyer who lobbied for the trucking, credit union and termite industries, so there was always a small barrier between us. No big deal, but I had trouble getting too close to somebody whose livelihood and success depended on influencing me and the other officials of the State of Oklahoma. Also, he had grown up in Stillwater, which was basketball-crazy, and I was more interested in baseball.

I had found it difficult to become really close to my fellow state officials too. They were all my friends, but on the other hand, no they weren't. Just as Buffalo Joe said. And that included Joe. How could anybody be friends with a governor? Luther Wallace, the speaker of the house, was smart and honest, and I enjoyed talking legislation and work with him. But there wasn't really anything that personal about it. Not yet, at least.

It had already happened with C., of course. And now it had been sixteen days since I had seen him. At first I told myself I did not care if I ever saw him again. But I knew that feeling would go away. Our friendship would survive the Sooner Spy spectacle. It might not have survived a full-blown Thunderbird sign spectacle, but fortunately it did not come to that.

I could tell his secretary was relieved and delighted that I was finally on the phone again. Her name was Marie. Marie Joan Thomasson of Sand Springs. She, like Janice Alice, clearly believed it was good that C. and I had each other as playmates.

C. came on the phone in a split second.

"How about some lunch?" I asked.

"I'm ready," he said.

"McDonald's or Burger King?"

"Your call," he said.

"Burger King."

"See you downstairs at twelve twenty-two."

"Twelve twenty-two?"

"Precisely."

Just like old times.

"Downstairs" meant at the capitol's west parking lot entrance.

I was there at 12:22 precisely. So was C. I joined him in

the backseat of his black Lincoln. Smitty, OBI special agent Smith, was driving the car, which was as much a legend as C. It was equipped with metal plate and bulletproof glass and an assortment of exotic firearms and tear gas and lights and radios and flares and megaphones—everything a person could possibly ever need in any kind of emergency or tragedy.

It was awkward and difficult between us at first. We went to the Burger King north of the capitol on Lincoln Boulevard. Our first words were mostly about what I was going to order and who was going to pay for it. He had his usual, a Whopper with everything, a large order of fries and a shake. I had the same except a Dr Pepper instead of milk. And I let him pay for it. For old times' sake. Brother Walt would have called it part of the healing process.

C. asked about Buffalo Joe's return to Oklahoma power. I told him about the Sell Oklahoma idea.

"The Chip's a raving lunatic," C. said. "He's also stupid. Instead of just selling it to the Japs, he should have a big international auction on TV. Invite everybody to play. Let the Arabs and the French and the Germans and the Texans and the Arkies and all the rest bid the prices up. It could be a remake of the big Oklahoma land rush."

It made me laugh. The only thing about C. that wasn't gray was his sense of humor. He could always make me laugh. Usually by laying into somebody. Somebody like Buffalo Joe.

He wanted to know about Tommy Walt and how his restaurant grease collection business was coming. I thanked him again for getting the Oklahoma City PD to act against the grease pirates. And I told him about Tommy Walt's acquisition and expansion plans.

"Well, you really do have to hand it to the kid, Mack," he said. "There aren't many people who could see a grand opportunity in hustling old grease from restaurants. Henry Ford and H. L. Hunt probably started the same way."

"Cars and oil are different from old grease from Colonel Sanders."

"Precisely."

I asked what he thought about The Golden Collection Plate as a name for Tommy Walt's business. He said it was a stupid idea and suggested I stay out of it.

I had been busy eating and had not paid any attention to where we were. My lunch trips with C. were seldom to anywhere. Smitty, or whoever was driving, just took off from the McDonald's or the Burger King and by keeping a good eye on the backseat tried to time things to end up back at the capitol shortly after we finished eating.

But the car came to a solid halt now. It was too soon to conclude things. I looked outside. We were in front of the National Motor Coach Museum.

"I had a feeling you wanted to talk very privately," C. said. "I thought maybe we could go for a walk around in here."

We got out of the car with what was left of our lunch and walked over to a picnic table that Fred Rayburn had put out for the tourists who never came. We didn't sit down. We just stood there and took our final bites and sips. Like good citizens, we tossed the leftover trash into a can and went inside.

I could go to that museum every day and never get bored. There are some things that must be seen again and again to be enjoyed. The little old American Buslines man was there again. But nobody else. C. and I stopped at a display

of magazine advertisements from the thirties and forties—
The Saturday Evening Post, Collier's, Liberty, National Geographic and others. They had true-to-life colored drawings of majestic Greyhound and Trailways buses speeding to their destinations through majestic canyons, majestic sandy beaches and majestic skyscrapers. Smiling passengers of all ages were depicted enjoying themselves in the hands of what the ads called "the world's best and safest drivers." I looked again at my favorite from the January 22, 1938, *Saturday Evening Post*. It was a full-page drawing of a new Greyhound Super Coach, one of the first luxury over-the-road buses with the motor in back instead of up front as in cars and trucks. There was a smiling handsome driver in a Sam Browne belt, britches and leather leggings talking to a group of passengers in front of the bus. One passenger had a set of skis on his shoulder. There were also a well-dressed young woman, a well-dressed middle-aged couple, a well-dressed elderly man with a cane holding the hand of a well-dressed little girl. Across the top in large black type, the ad said: "Ride with Us in This $20,000 Automobile." The small print below said: " 'A $20,000 automobile,' you say—'Why, even the snootiest foreign-built limousine doesn't cost that much money. How can *I* afford to travel in such a car?' " There were close-ups of features that "not even the swankiest foreign-built limousine" could match: Four-position reclining seats. Diffused tubular lighting. Healthful heating, ventilation. Long wheelbase for easy riding.

C. faked interest in the display for a couple of minutes. Then he said: "This is your party, Mack. You called. I hope it was just to make up and go on. Is that it?"

"Yes, that's it," I said. "The Sooner Spy thing is done and

over. It was rough, but the water has gone under the bridge and out to sea."

We ambled by the little cast-iron buses and around behind one of the two ticket counters in the place. This one Fred had found in the old bus depot in Humboldt, Tennessee. It was made in a heavy dark wood and had "Gulf Transport Company" and "Dixie Greyhound Lines" engraved on the front. A cut-glass window had a "Tickets—Information" sign over it.

C. pointed to a ticket validator on the counter. "What's this?" he asked.

"Watch." I took a piece of paper out of my billfold and demonstrated. I stuck the paper inside the validator and then banged the top down. Whack! A one-and-a-half-inch-square imprint was on the paper. "Altoona, Kansas" it said at the top. There was a date in the center. "Southern Kansas," for Southern Kansas Stage Lines, was across the bottom. It was not a particularly spectacular achievement. It did not surprise me when C. looked at it and said nothing.

"There are a couple of factual matters I would like to clear up, though," I said, putting the validator back in its proper position.

His gray eyes narrowed and zeroed in on me. "No, Mack. No factual matters are going to be cleared up. No. Let it rest. Please. Like you say, it's over and done."

"C., Art Pennington was not the spy. Bill Hagood is. He still is there in Utoka. I figured it out."

He smiled. And shook his head. Like saying, You are crazy, Mack.

"It was the *Oklahoma!* singing that gave it away. Collins said at dinner at the Park Plaza the KGB defector loved

Oklahoma! I found out at that Sturant thing that Art Pennington did not. And later I discovered it was Hagood who loved and sang the words from *Oklahoma!* I figured it out because Collins made a mistake. So not just one-eyed lieutenant governors and one-eared OBI directors make mistakes by talking too much." And I told him about the bank and JackieMart records and the phone call.

"Okay, let's say you're right. What difference does it make?" C. said.

"The difference is, Calvin the Russian Killer murdered the wrong man. Y'all let me steer him to the wrong man. Right?"

"Not me. I didn't know either. I thought Pennington was the defector too. That's why I gave you that stupid 'Ask Jackie' clue. Collins always told me it was the guy at the JackieMart. Those people don't really trust anybody to know everything. That's how it works. I don't mind. I'm a professional. But look at how it turned out. The Russian goes away thinking he's killed the defector. The real defector remains where he is, forever protected because the Russians think he's dead. Add in turning a young KGB killer into a spy for us, and you have quite a deal."

"Yes, sir," I said.

He turned and we started walking again. We went by two driver's seats. One was from a 1929 Faegol, the other from a 1937 ACF. In front of the seats were steering wheels from each of the buses mounted on shafts bolted into heavy wood pedestals, so you could sit and get the feel of driving a bus. C. nodded toward the seats. He took the Faegol. I sat down in the ACF seat. They were side by side, only a yard apart.

Now the smile was gone. "Mack, I commend you for your

brilliance. But the information you have is deadly. If Collins and his people even had a hint you had figured it out, they would go bananas. You could blow one of the best little operations like this they have ever pulled off. You haven't told anybody else, have you?"

"Certainly not. And I never will."

"Never?"

"That's right."

"I believe you, Mack. Because of what happened, Collins would never believe you, but I do. I probably shouldn't, but I do. You got burned once; you are not going to go back for seconds."

"Did anybody happen to ask Calvin the Russian Killer why he picked on me in the first place? Why he came to that Oklahoma Southeastern commencement?"

A slight pink cast came into C.'s gray face. He grabbed the Faegol steering wheel and gave it a slight turn to the left.

"Well, yes," he said. "Somebody asked. He looked at a lot of files before he came to Oklahoma, and in them were newspaper stories about you and me and our friendship. He said he took a chance on friendship. On the fact that I probably knew where Pronnikov was, and that if I knew then you could probably find out, because we were friends."

"Calvin was one smart young man. Too bad he didn't really go to Oklahoma Southeastern. If I'm right, then who was Pennington?"

"I have no idea." He turned the wheel back to the right.

"I believe he was a U.S. agent of some kind. Placed there to hand-hold and keep a lookout on Hagood. He was the contact Collins talked about."

"Wrong. The contact was another guy. I *do* know that.

He was there before Hagood and Pennington came to Utoka. I don't know who he was—or is."

"So that makes three. Three spies in Utoka, Oklahoma? Unbelievable!"

He looked at his watch. "I have a citizen-kook meeting this afternoon. Some natural-gas tycoon from Enid wants to give us a half-million-dollar private grant to buy armored cars and run down drug dealers and cigarette smugglers. All I have to do is promise to hire his grandson as a special agent and assign him to the Enid office."

"I returned the Thunderbird bus depot sign."

"Returned it? How?"

"The same way I took it."

"Breaking and entering is against the law no matter what you break and enter for. You are a most unusual lieutenant governor of Oklahoma, Mack."

"I'd sure like to have your copy of that Utoka PD report on the first burglary."

His face got a little pink in it again. He pushed the Faegol's horn button in the center of the steering wheel. Nothing happened. The horn was not hooked up.

"Haven't got one. There never was one."

"What did you have in your hand, then?"

"A blank piece of paper."

"How did you know about the sign?"

"I have my sources. Now that's it. Got to go."

No Utoka PD report? Something was screwy. But right now I had one more item of business with C.

"There's something else," I said. "I think you should know that I believe Art Pennington is not really dead."

My good right eye was on him as tightly as possible. The pink disappeared.

"That's crazy! Absolutely Chip crazy, Mack. Come on."

I told him Brother Walt had found there was no record or any other sign that he was brought to Dallas.

"That means not one single solitary thing. They probably took him off somewhere else. Relax."

His reaction seemed honest.

"This is not another one of those secrets that the lieutenant governor does not need to know?"

"No, Mack. No. If I thought Pennington was alive I would say so. That would be a great ending. Nobody got hurt. A super deal. But forget it. You saw the real movie. You saw those gunshots. You saw him fall back on that floor. Come on!"

"He could have been wearing a bulletproof vest. I am sure there are ways to stage those things."

"Mack, no. The man died. If he was an agent, and maybe he was, then those are the breaks. He knew what he was in for when he got involved in this business. Relax. . . ."

"I just do not believe the United States of America would allow a Russian to kill an American citizen like that. I just do not believe it."

C. was on his feet now. He stuck out his right hand. I took it.

"Mack, you are a good man. The very best. Believe what you want to. I will go right ahead believing what I want to, and we'll never know the real truth. Let's go. My appointment's at one-thirty."

On the way back to the capitol, we talked about Nixon and the Cardinals and Jackie's decision to expand JackieMart into Arkansas.

As I got out of the car he grabbed my right hand again.

"Thanks, Mack. McDonald's next week?"

"Your call."

I went inside, resumed my duties as lieutenant governor of Oklahoma, and started wondering how they found out about my burglary and who in the world that third man could have been?

After a while I figured it out. The information about the burglary came from the Utoka Sparrow. Which meant he was the third spy, the guy who was there before Hagood and Pennington.

I could not imagine what the CIA saw in such a jerk.